The
12 Yogic Principles
for
Making Marriages Work

A dynamic and charismatic personality, **Dr Hansaji J. Yogendra** is the wife of yoga guru Dr Jayadeva Yogendra and the director of The Yoga Institute. She has dedicated her life to teaching yoga as a way of life in a completely practical way at the institute. She is revered not only for her outstanding accomplishments but also for the noble example that she has set for the yoga community. She is best known for her involvement in the popular television series Yoga for Better Living first aired in 1980.

Hansaji has been recognized for her contribution to women's health through the award presented by the Scheme for Promotion of Academic and Research Collaboration (SPARC). She has conducted many seminars and given lectures in India and abroad. She has also authored many articles and books on yoga such as *Yoga for All*. She and Dr Jayadeva were invited by the National Council for Educational Research and Training (NCERT) to formulate a syllabus on yoga education for schools nationwide. Hansaji is the country's only lady yoga guru to be invited by Prime Minister Narendra Modi to grace the first International Day of Yoga on 21 June 2015 in New Delhi. Under her astute guidance, The Yoga Institute won the Prime Minister's Award for Outstanding Contribution for the Promotion and Development of Yoga in 2018.

Connect with the institute at:
Facebook: theyogainstituteofficial;
Instagram: theyogainstituteofficial; Twitter: tyi_official;
YouTube: theyogainstituteofficial;
Email: hansaji@theyogainstitute.org;
Website: www.theyogainstitute.org

Also by the Author

Yoga for All

The
12 Yogic Principles
for
Making Marriages Work

Hansaji J. Yogendra

Published by
Rupa Publications India Pvt. Ltd 2019
7/16, Ansari Road, Daryaganj
New Delhi 110002

Sales centres:

Allahabad Bengaluru Chennai
Hyderabad Jaipur Kathmandu
Kolkata Mumbai

Copyright © The Yoga Institute 2019

Photographs by Nirali Manek
Illustrations by Aryka Fyzee

The views and opinions expressed in this book are the
author's own and the facts are as reported by her which
have been verified to the extent possible, and the publishers
are not in any way liable for the same.

All rights reserved.
No part of this publication may be reproduced, transmitted,
or stored in a retrieval system, in any form or by any means,
electronic, mechanical, photocopying, recording or otherwise,
without the prior permission of the publisher.

ISBN: 978-93-5333-595-3

First impression 2019

10 9 8 7 6 5 4 3 2 1

The moral right of the author has been asserted.

This book is sold subject to the condition that it shall not,
by way of trade or otherwise, be lent, resold, hired out, or otherwise
circulated, without the publisher's prior consent, in any form of binding or
cover other than that in which it is published.

*This book is dedicated to Dr Jayadeva Yogendra
who was the epitome of a true householder yogi.*

CONTENTS

Foreword		*ix*
Preface		*xi*
Introduction		*xv*
1.	Discovering Yourself through Yoga	1
2.	Practising Yoga for a Happy Married Life	13
3.	Learning Acceptance through Yoga	26
4.	Building Trust through Yoga	35
5.	Communicating Effectively through Pranayama	47
6.	Developing Love, Intimacy through Yoga	56
7.	Managing Expectations through Yoga	64
8.	Conquering the Ego through Yoga	74
9.	Mastering Parenting Skills through Yoga	86
10.	Achieving Mental Balance through Yoga	99
11.	Managing Finances through Yoga	109
12.	Staying Detached and Cultivating Friendship in Marriage	119
Testimonials		127
In Gratitude		131

FOREWORD

In today's fast paced world where marriages are breaking down at the slightest of stress, this latest book, *The 12 Yogic Principles for Making Marriages Work*, has tips for both the partners in life. It not only guides them on how to make their lives more meaningful but also encourages them to live it in the best possible way.

Marriage is a wonderful journey between two experienced and enlightened souls where false egos many a time are the root cause of break-ups. The simple yogic wisdom and practical guidelines suggested in this book will help in eliminating the cause of break-ups and also benefit the couple in attaining an elevated spiritual state.

The 12 Yogic Principles for Making Marriages Work is a timely gift in today's world as a healing touch for those who find life incompatible after marriage. They say, 'Marriages are made in heaven', but reading this book will definitely bring the real paradise in one's life.

My salutations to The Yoga Institute and its team ably led by the humble icon—Hansaji for thinking about today's generation and giving them this beautiful gift to experience harmonious relationships.

Musically,
Pandit Shiv Kumar Sharma,
Padma Vibhushan awardee

PREFACE

Just like a lot of films have a Part 1 and a Part 2, life too has a Part 2, and it begins with marriage. Everyone acknowledges this and hence it is not surprising that this new phase of life is celebrated everywhere with prayers and pomp. Marriage signifies that a man and a woman have come of age (ideally) and are ready to embark on their own journey (hopefully!). The union could have the blessings of the couple's parents, but the journey is the couple's own—a voyage of life with its own joys and pleasures, sorrows and pains. How many people prepare themselves for this journey? You prepare yourself for your school and college examinations, you put in years of learning and gathering skills for career development, you do the necessary spadework for job interviews, you prepare yourself for practically everything important in your life, but you don't bother to prepare yourself emotionally for the most crucial phase of your life.

The 12 Yogic Principles for Making Marriages Work helps one to be marriage-ready, not just wedding-ready. It is important to be prepared for the most significant phase of one's life because all of us are imperfect, all of us have picked up some baggage on the way, all of us have our egos to grapple with, and it is our efforts and successes at overcoming these challenges that help us evolve. And when there are two people involved, there will be twice as many challenges and twice as many rewards. A bird with two wings flies faster than a bird with one. All of us want to become better, fuller, happier human beings, but this requires effort and learning.

One doesn't have to be a genius to know how to conduct oneself and the principles are the same for all situations, whether it's an interaction with a stranger or a neighbour or a friend or a colleague or a relative. It's particularly true in the case of a close bond like marriage. 'Do unto others as you would have them do unto you' should be your guideline in marriage. Isn't this common sense? In a marital relationship, you should be just as caring, considerate, gentle, kind, respectful to the other person as you would like the other to be to you, yet many a time you forget this golden rule while you are busy chasing the big things in life. Slow down, smell flowers and be nice to others. Yoga, mistaken and misunderstood by the world as a set of postures (or asanas) for achieving fitness, can help you cultivate the values needed desperately today to live in harmony with not only yourself but also your life partner. By understanding and implementing these practical twelve yogic principles, a couple will be able experience a harmonious and long-lasting relationship.

There are many yoga postures and facets of yoga philosophy that teach the importance of calmness, honesty, non-covetousness, contentment and other positive values, and, more importantly, the benefits of cultivating these values. Why can't couples imbibe these values? If you don't acknowledge their importance now, they will come knocking on your door someday. If you don't learn balance, nature will force you to learn it someday. And the knock on the door from a disgruntled life partner will come first.

In this day and age, living independently from each other also takes away connection and joy from the relationship. Couples must function as a team when it comes to parenting, performing household duties, managing financial responsibilities and fulfilling social commitments. A couple needs to be in tandem with each other at both emotional and intellectual levels. Based on the foundation of key yogic principles, a successful marriage is driven by unconditional love as well as unwavering commitment and trust. A successful marriage is driven by unconditional love as well as unwavering commitment and trust. Small gestures go a long way to strengthen a marriage.

Dr Jayadeva, my husband, would always keep a throat lozenge in his pocket whenever we were giving lectures as he was aware that I often needed it during the long hours of lecturing. In the same way, to show concern for a partner, for example, if a wife knows that her husband is forgetful, she must ensure that they celebrate their wedding anniversary happily. She can do this by reminding her husband well in advance and make necessary arrangements herself instead of waiting for him to forget and then pounce on him, losing the plot completely. A happy family life is at the heart of Indian culture.

I hope that readers will find in this book some of the wisdom that yoga has to offer and apply these teachings to their lives, especially in their marital relationship. The Indian cultural ethos believes that life is sacred and every human being is unique. If you hold on to this perspective, you can learn to accept another person's faults instead of trying to change him/her. This is the key to a lasting relationship and marital bliss.

INTRODUCTION

In the olden days, a marriage that didn't last was the talk of the town. How things have changed now! It's the marriage that lasts that gets talked about most now. Many wonder what the happy couple is doing right and where they can buy the magic wand for long-lasting marriages.

There is no magic wand.

It's a skill that has to be learnt just like skydiving or cycling or swimming. Only this one is a little more challenging. It involves learning all the things your parents, teachers, elders and good books advised you to learn when you were young. It's all the things you either thought you already knew or would pick up along the way like goodness, kindness, compassion, patience. You didn't pick them up because you got busy with other things—like life, for example.

The 12 Yogic Principles for Making Marriages Work is a definitive guidebook for all those who want to attain the highest potential of their relationship by building it on the rich and strong foundation of yoga philosophy. The simple, fundamental principles listed here will enhance the quality of the emotional connection between the couple and their respect for each other.

With the practice of yoga way of living, those involved in a relationship can discover themselves; practice yoga; learn acceptance; build trust; communicate effectively; develop love and intimacy; manage expectations; conquer the ego; master parenting skills; achieve mental balance; manage finances and eventually stay detached and cultivate friendship in marriage.

It's never too late.

THE YOGA WAY OF LIVING

Yoga can help you cultivate and imbibe all these qualities. 'Cultivating' may be the wrong word actually. You already possess these qualities—you have just become desensitized over the years and have forgotten how to invoke them. The grim business of making a living has done that to you. But if you have picked up this book, then you are heading the right way.

Now you're probably wondering how a set of asanas can help you rediscover yourself. They can't because there's much more to yoga than just asanas. Asanas are one of the steps in Ashtanga yoga or the eightfold path based on the *Yoga Sutras* compiled by Patanjali prior to 400 BC. The *Yoga Sutras* of Patanjali are a collection of 196 Indian sutras on the theory and practice of yoga.

Ashtanga yoga comprises the following eight steps: yamas (don'ts), niyamas (observances), asanas (postures), pranayamas (breathing techniques), pratyahara (first step to internalization), dharana (holding one's attention), dhyana (concentration) and samadhi (prolonged concentration).

Yamas are rules of the moral code. These include ahimsa (non-violence), satya (truthfulness), asteya (non-stealing), brahmacharya (moderation) and aparigraha (non-possessiveness).

Niyamas are good habits and observances. Saucha (purity), santosha (contentment), tapas (discipline), svadhyaya (spiritual studies and study of the self), and Ishvara pranidhana (surrender to God) are the five niyamas.

Asanas are different physical exercises or postures for

keeping one's body fit and comfortable. Pranayama includes breathing techniques that help to control one's prana or the vital life force. By the way of breathing, one can also control one's thought process.

Pratyahara teaches one to be objective in life and while dharana refers to concentration, dhyana is the practice of meditation or contemplation leading to the uninterrupted flow of concentration. Samadhi is becoming one with the subject of meditation and merging with the Divine.

If a couple follows the yoga way of living, the egoistic tendencies of both will diminish over time and they will become more humble.

Asanas are synonymous to yoga in this day and age, but yoga is much more than just asanas.

YOU CAN DO YOUR ASANAS AND EAT PIZZA TOO!

Asanas can help you stay fit, which is no doubt very important, but a straight spine or firm calf muscles are of little use to diffuse the real or imagined pain that you experience in your marriage. Asanas also help practitioners stay seated in a meditation posture for a prolonged duration of time. No, you don't have to go the icy caves in the Himalayas to do so! It is not just your body that requires your attention; you have to watch your mind and thoughts as well. This book will help dispel the biggest misconception about yoga—that yoga and asanas are interchangeable.

The eight steps of yoga are basically prescriptions on how to engage with the world outside and embark on a journey within, to live in peace and harmony with one's spouse, children, parents, neighbours and pets. And you don't have to lie down on a bed of nails like exotic yogis to attain self-realization. You can continue to eat pizza (not every day though, and go easy on the cheese) because it is not as dangerous as the many books that exoticize yoga and yogis for the consumption of the international audience.

ONE-SIZE-FITS-ALL?

The market is full of books, mostly from the West, on how to make marriages and relationships work, on parenting and other topics. No doubt there is much to be learnt from these books, but it has to be kept in mind that they are aimed largely at a Western audience. Urban India is definitely leaning towards the West, which is a more individualistic society compared to the Indian society, which is collectivist. For the West, 'freedom' has always meant the 'freedom to indulge'; for the East, 'freedom' implies 'freedom from indulgence'. There is little doubt that the East and the West have different outlooks on life and different approaches. Both are distinctly different in matters of upbringing, social interaction, child-rearing and so on and this difference naturally pervades all areas of an individual's life. Relationships and marriages, like people all over the world, are different in their own ways, and it would be unwise to serve a one-size-fits-all solution for the challenges couples face in the vast global space. India has its own culture, traditions, customs and rituals, which if understood properly can breathe new life into its citizens. It is with this in mind that The Yoga Institute has decided to bring out this book.

THE GITA AS A SELF-HELP BOOK

Instead of looking at the Bhagavad Gita as a book to be dressed in holy red cloth and left to gather dust in a temple, if one looks at it as a manual for self-development and self-discovery—much can be gained by reading and understanding it. Patanjali's *Yoga Sutras* can offer the world insights into the workings of the mind, which would benefit individuals or couples immensely. It would be a big mistake not to tap into this vast bank of knowledge and apply it to one's life.

The Bhagavad Gita throws light on duality, as each human is made up of consciousness (purusha) and matter (prakriti). The scripture details the changing quality of prakriti. So when change occurs in your life, accept it and do your best. Change is the only constant. The same person who once expressed love immensely will not do so with the same intensity at other times. Yoga philosophy, which teaches one to maintain a balanced state of mind, helps one to cope with life and its various challenges. In the Bhagavad Gita, Lord Krishna defines yoga as '*Samatvam yoga uchyate* (Yoga is a balanced state)'.

THE YOGA INSTITUTE'S PHILOSOPHY REGARDING MARRIAGE

Indians have foolishly ignored the ancient spiritual wisdom of the scriptures, unless it is validated by the West. What a pity!

Yoga and ancient Indian philosophy have believed since time immemorial that the key to happiness lies with the individual. The special couples classes held at The Yoga Institute, a government-recognized non-profit organization known as the oldest organized yoga centre in the world, guide married, both old and young, couples through the challenges of life. The case studies mentioned in this book are real, but the names have been changed to protect the identity of individuals. If you have met your partner, it's high time you met yourself. This book helps you take the right step in that direction.

1

DISCOVERING YOURSELF THROUGH YOGA

Marriage and, later, children bring about tectonic shifts in the lives of people. Total commitment is a must, and this requires digging one's heels in to stay the course and 'learning' to live happily with one another. The operative word here is 'learning'. Regardless of the class the person belongs to, influential mothers and fathers will be unable to buy and ensure happiness, success, or even pass marks for their wards in wedlock; one has to go through the grind before being awarded the degree.

CHANGE BEGINS WITH YOU

The first few years are years of learning, and in these years, if you are sensitive enough, while you get to know your partner, you certainly will get to learn more about yourself. It is one thing to believe that one is magnanimous or kind or selfless when one is single, but after marriage all these claims are tested and a person is stripped of his or her self-deluding notions and forced to see oneself for what one really is. That is when one realizes that changes will have to be made.

It's pointless trying to change the world around you if you cannot start with yourself. It is only when you start with yourself that you will realize that it's extremely difficult to change oneself and then, if you are smart enough, you will realize the futility of trying to change another person.

Shri Yogendra, founder of The Yoga Institute, used to narrate a story often: Anagha requested her guru to advise her young son to give up his addiction to sweets, but he requested her to wait for a fortnight. After two weeks, she returned to him with her son. Clearing his throat, her teacher sternly told the boy, 'You must give up your addiction to sweets, too much of anything is not good for you.' Anagha was surprised. After the boy left to play outside, she remonstrated with the teacher for making her wait. 'You could have said that two weeks ago when I brought him here.'

'Two weeks ago I did not have the right to tell him,' her teacher replied, 'I was addicted to sweets myself. I felt it would be appropriate to advise him when I had overcome the challenge myself.'

Perhaps the only way to bring about a change in another person close to you is to change yourself first. Only if he or she has the hide of a buffalo will the person not be touched and moved by your success—it might even motivate him or her to attempt to do the same.

YOGA TO THE RESCUE!

As this is a book on marriage from the perspective of yoga, it is essential to delve a little deeper into their connect. Could yoga bring joy and balance in a marital relationship? Yes. How? Yoga helps to bring a balance in one's own life, once this is achieved one is able to harmonize with one's own environment. But the word 'yoga' has to be understood properly. To know what yoga is, it is important to first know what it is not. The word has been misunderstood by many over the years. A person advised to follow the path of yoga or spirituality is more often than not intimidated by it because of the popular idea of yoga is associated with people either standing or sitting in strange or gravity-defying postures or waking up at the crack of dawn to chant mantras and sing bhajans in temples or fasting or growing a beard and heading for the mountains or giving up one's favourite food. In short, leading a stoic life of grim determination. The West has played an important role in exotifying yogis and babas for popular consumption. While one cannot deny that such people exist, it is possible to walk the path of yoga without living a life of austerity.

Yoga will help you to cultivate a sound mind and body. Such a person will be an asset to society, the nation and also the perfect co-driver to navigate any relationship. The cultivation of a sound body and mind requires a certain amount of effort on the individual's part. Some call this the road of spirituality but, in modern parlance, it is the road to self-growth or personality development and yoga provides a more holistic approach towards it.

So much for the big picture.

A closer look at yoga reveals the details, that is, the lifestyle, attitudes, values, habits and diet essential for the development of a balanced personality.

Yoga advocates a certain kind of food that is wholesome, simple, fresh, nutritious and easy to digest because a healthy individual is naturally more capable of facing the vicissitudes of life. In yoga parlance, sattvic food (for example, fresh fruits and vegetables) keeps one light in both body and mind, rajasic food (for example, hot substances, such as sharp spices or strong herbs or stimulants like coffee and tea, meat and fish, eggs, salt and chocolate) is that which makes one restless and tamasic food is stale or unnatural or unhealthy (for example, alcohol and tobacco). You might be required to give up junk food, but you don't have to give up delicious food. As people are becoming increasingly aware of the dangers of the wrong kind of food, they are adding healthy and delicious food to their diet. Recipes for these or information about where they are available can be found easily on the internet. Therefore, all fears of giving up delicious food are totally unfounded.

Yoga also advocates non-materialism, but this has to be understood properly. For a person living in a city, earning a living can be a struggle, but yoga doesn't suggest that you give it up. It just teaches one that a mad pursuit of wealth is unhealthy for both mind and body, and if this lesson is not learnt early in life then you will be left to ponder over it by lying in a hospital bed, recovering from the damage you have caused yourself. The newspapers these days are replete with stories of young men and women suffering maladies like blood pressure, heart attacks, diabetes, which once were exclusively dealt by the older population.

By advocating introspection, yoga actually equips you to face the uphill task of earning a living bravely and cheerfully. This does call for a certain degree of discipline (another much misunderstood word), self-restraint (yet another) and mindfulness.

In the language of yoga, the entire material world is made up of three gunas (qualities): sattva, rajas and tamas, and everyone is a blend of two or more of these qualities with one of them dominant. A sattva-dominant personality is generally a peaceful and cheerful person; a rajasic person is aggressive, active, tense (a Type A personality in the language of psychology) and a tamasic person is dull and lethargic. The aim of yoga is to help an individual with techniques, for both body and mind, to attain a sattvic state. A person with a sound mind in a sound body is naturally a well-rounded individual and also a good team player. These qualities then, naturally, make it easier to attain harmony in relationships.

The layman will be astonished if he consults a yoga teacher for some advice on relationships and is told to learn a breathing technique or song as a solution. How on earth can a breathing technique rescue a relationship? And considering how poor most people are at singing, it could only hurt a relationship. When Nayan, a forty-four-year-old incapacitated by arthritis and often depressed, consulted Dr Jayadeva, yoga guru, researcher, author, educator and former president of The Yoga Institute, she was advised to team up with a group of friends to play a game of cards regularly. It was a simple solution and actually took care of the depression.

Chatting, joking, playing games, singing together, being nice to each other, helping one another are some of the small things that can add big value to your life and relationships as they did to Nayan's. That didn't fix her arthritis, but the mind affects the body—this has been proved—and a calm, balanced, pleasant state of mind helped her to put her aches and pains aside, and made her a more amicable person than the angry and disturbed person she was. Breathing techniques help you to stay calm in situations that would easily disturb most people; simple meditation techniques can help develop a broader vision, which in turn makes it possible to see situations in the proper perspective instead of exploding in anger.

Yamas and niyamas like ahimsa and satya teach you to be gentle, honest and transparent. Yoga teaches you not only asanas and pranayamas, but also the importance of diet, recreation, good habits and positive thinking. The thoughts you think make you the person you are, and this further determines the choices you make, the experiences you have and the people you attract. The strategy is to change your attitude—the goal is to become a better individual and a better team player.

They say that a wise person learns from his mistakes but a wiser one learns from others' mistakes. Yoga introduces you to the sacred and divine within you, and only a person who has met the sacred within himself can recognize the same in others and thus become capable of honouring relationships like marriage.

You can choose to learn all this after a long and tiresome journey riddled with wrongs and regrets about hurting yourself, your spouse/partner, family, friends and others close to you or you could learn before making the mistakes. The choice is yours.

THE YOGA ASANA PRACTICE

BEGIN WITH A PLAN

Set a goal by writing out a plan—this should be your first step. It will help you to achieve clarity in thought and action. To set a goal is to do something 'at will'. This is the beginning of yoga. It is to take charge of your mind, intellect and body. This means that from now on you will be responsible for yourself. This responsibility and actions therefrom will ensure appropriate results. However, here the aim is not to seek results immediately but to concentrate on effective practice.

FIX A TIME

Such a plan will have to 'fit' in comfortably with your daily schedule. At the outset, you may decide to allocate at least thirty to forty minutes of undisturbed time for yoga practice, considering it as a 'duty to oneself'. Later you can increase the duration to about an hour.

The best time for yoga practice is in the morning before breakfast. You can choose any time during the day that suits you if you miss a morning session. An important idea in yoga is to ensure that the calmness created during the practice session is extended throughout the day and infuses every activity.

There will be days when you may not have the time to practise yoga or you may be unwell. Do not fret or feel guilty as accepting situations and circumstances is also part of yoga practice. However, this should not be an excuse not to practice!

On such days, practise for a shorter duration. During such occasions you can choose one or two asanas (standing, sitting and supine) and perform just one or two repetitions so that in a short time span you are putting your body through all the movements. Take care to warm up properly.

Once you have decided the time you are going to devote to your practice, stay with the time as much as possible and maintain a record. Of course, be flexible as rigidity causes more problems. A record will help in future reflections.

OTHER SUGGESTIONS

It is best to practise asanas when your bowels are clean. You may drink a glass or two of water in room temperature or slightly warmer before commencing asanas. Clothes made of breathable natural fabric are the ideal yoga wear.

Physical practice sessions are not recommended on a full stomach. So wait a couple of hours after a heavy meal, then commence your practice.

To ensure that yoga just doesn't remain a set of mere physical exercises, Dr Jayadeva added bhavas (emotions) to enrich them and keep the students interested. The four bhavas are:

1. Dharma (duty),
2. Jnana (knowledge/concentration),
3. Vairagya (detachment) and
4. Aishwarya (feeling godlike).

The practice of dharma, jnana, vairagya and aishwarya will lead to self-development and a positive transformation of your personality. The integrated practice of the four positive bhavas will encompass every action you perform in your life, irrespective of how insignificant or great the action may be. Every practice has its corresponding effect within the physiology of your being. These effects relate to the four bhavas.

The presence of one bhava in a practice session is always more pronounced than the other three. Thus, it may be that one bhava is predominant while the others play a subsidiary or supporting role.

For example, meditative postures are categorized in the dharma bhava as its predominant bhava, yet they do give rise to knowledge (jnana bhava). They create detachment from irrelevant thoughts (vairagya bhava) and sitting in that posture for a longer duration encourages self-discipline and strength (aishwarya bhava). While most asanas for extremities enhance the jnana bhava, all forward-bending asanas help to reinforce the vairagya bhava. The heart-opening, back-bending asanas strengthen the aishwarya bhava.

When the bhavas are applied to physical practice, the mind works in tandem with the body to create a holistic and more intense effect. A technique that is practised in isolation could well be just another form of exercise!

As the mind tends to constantly wander, the bhavas help students to arrest the wandering mind and gain more from an asana than they would otherwise.

The dharma bhava involves taking responsibility for all of your actions through self-discipline, self-motivation, self-direction and self-commitment. All other bhavas fall in step, such that without the practice of dharma, the other bhavas become insignificant.

Through the practice of dharma, jnana arises. Keen awareness and realization unfolds as you become more fine-tuned to your actions and relations to the world outside. A deep awareness of your body–mind relationship will help you to manage the outside world. Jnana will help you to develop one-pointedness. It is increasing concentration and focus while doing any activity and represents awareness and wisdom, not mere informative knowledge of the world.

Objectivity is the keynote of the notion of vairagya. Often misunderstood as relinquishing of the activities and beauty of life, it is more about a 'mind-state' that is beyond greed and personal attachments that bind one into endless misery. It is to refrain from accumulating a mountain of thoughts that form a formidable baggage. Vairagya also inhibits excessive hoarding of material possessions.

The practice of one's own dharma ensures that jnana arises, which enables true vairagya of the mind to be instated. It is only when one has sincerely practised the dharma bhava, which has given rise to the jnana and vairagya bhavas, that there arises supreme faith, assurance, goodwill and decisiveness. The aishwarya bhava is reflected in the determination, strength, courage, self-confidence and power of the 'will' of the individual which arises from perceptive wisdom.

The aishwarya bhava brings forth humility and compassion as qualities that develop from a fullness of wisdom. It eradicates pride, vanity, arrogance and makes the individual a strong and powerful being who rises above the ordinary.

The bhavas are also a part of pranayamas and kriyas. The jnana bhava is predominant in the practice of the pranayamas and the aishwarya bhava is infused in the practice of the kriyas, with the other bhavas playing subsidiary roles.

Forward-bending asanas like Yoga Mudra (refer to Chapter 8), for example, are to be done with the bhava of vairagya, while backward-bending asanas like Bhujangasana (refer to Chapter 7), are to be done with the bhava of aishwarya as an aid to increasing one's self-esteem. It must be understood that doing these asanas with the specific bhavas will not automatically make a person more detached or increase self-esteem or help in better concentration. An equal effort is required on the part of the student; the feelings have to be invoked, reflected and dwelt upon, and accompanied by an effort to understand the importance of these qualities and build them up in other areas of life as well.

For example, Bhujangasana alone will not increase your self-esteem, but accompanied by positive results from the efforts to do well at studies or at work, certainly will boost your self-esteem. If Musa, the Sufi mystic, had merely done Yoga Mudra, he would have gained a certain amount of vairagya, but he cultivated it consciously; he loved dry fruits, so he would lay out a feast of his favourite foods in front of him and then invite others to eat them while he watched. He cultivated self-restraint and detachment by not succumbing to the temptation of consuming his favourite foods.

Yoga teaches you to become focused and free by overcoming the weaknesses within you.

In a lighter vein:

'Make me one with everything,' the yogi announced as he walked into the pizza parlour. He received his pizza, put his 500-rupee note on the counter and waited patiently.

He continued to wait.

Finally, he told the cashier, 'I think you owe me change.'

'Change must come from within,' the cashier replied.

2

PRACTISING YOGA FOR A HAPPY MARRIED LIFE

Avi and Kavya were married with much fanfare. As usual, things were hunky-dory in the beginning, but, predictably, differences started to surface. Kavya's disapproval of Avi spending a lot of time with his college buddies was the main bone of contention between them. She was hurt that he didn't like to spend time with her. He did, but he also wanted to keep his friendships alive, and, naturally, he found her attitude stifling. When the children came along, he did justice to his role as a father, but he certainly was bothered by the fact that now he had even less time for his friends. He rapidly became irritable until one day he blew his top. He was scheduled to meet his friends to watch the India–Pakistan cricket match live on TV, and had been looking forward to this day—but Kavya fell ill on that very day. Now it fell on him to take over running the household, fetching the children from school as well as seeing to the myriad tasks that needed to be done. Meeting his friends was out of question. The match was a draw; no one lost the match but Avi lost his mood, his fuse and sulked for days on end.

MARRIAGE: A BLISSFUL STATE OF COMPLETENESS

Hum Aapke Hain Koun...!, one of the biggest grossers in the history of Bollywood, ran for over a hundred weeks. It showcased everything related to the traditional Indian wedding—song, dance, fun, glamour, good-looking men and women, appetizing food, great attire and also a nice little doggie. People loved it. The people in the film were happy, the people watching the film were happy too.

Indian weddings are known for their style, tradition and magnificence, and cynics often joke that fun ends on the day of the wedding—thereafter, real life takes over. Until then, everything was in control—the dates could be changed, the menu for guests could be changed, the car of choice could be hired, suits and gowns could be altered, but once the wedding is over, the bride and groom are faced with each other and the fact that now nothing major can be altered, either easily or quickly or peacefully.

A man and a woman are different in many aspects as a woman thinks from her heart and the man with his head. Thus one person's logic rules thinking, while the other's emotions may dominate more. Therefore, a person can become whole only when he or she develops both areas. Marriage enhances one's discipline, clarity, commitment, responsibility and most importantly, adaptability. Each partner learns to adjust and appreciate the other. A committed relationship like marriage helps one not to have a strong opinion but a strong commitment to gear up for every occurrence, every event in life. It makes one's sharp edges smoother to manoeuvre through the journey of life. Marriage helps one to see beyond one's own self and expand one's horizon. One becomes less self-centred. However, all this is not possible without a committed relationship like marriage. Human beings are meant to grow and multiply. No other species gets married, but a human being does.

Here is a very good example to drill the message through. When you dig forty feet into the ground, you may not find water. And if you keep digging forty feet at other spots, you may still not find water. But if you keep digging deeper in the same spot, chances are bright that you may strike a well of water.

A happy married life will help a person to reach a blissful state of completeness, and a happy person is an asset to society.

Just like Avi and Kavya's equation went through changes, all relationships go through the bump and grind of the long, winding, uneven road called marriage, and you might often catch yourself thinking, *This is not the person I married.* One presents one's best side in the early days of courtship, but everyone has more facets to them than they care to show. For example, a husband may not be willing to accept the fact that his wife earns more than him, and his wife may not be happy with the fact that he earns less than her. The constantly shifting dynamics of a society in the throes of rapid change can keep a couple on their toes, but this dance has to be learnt. It requires immense patience and very little room for the ego.

But first things first. Of course, you have to tick off some crucial boxes when choosing your life partner. Initially, you could be drawn to the superfluous aspects of your potential spouse, such as appearance, possessions (for example, model of the car, size of the house, bank balance) and other factors. To a certain extent, some of these factors are important, but it would be foolish to invest your life on this basis. The model of a car is important when you are picking a car, not when you are choosing your life partner. After the initial screening is completed, it makes perfect sense to spend some time with the person who could become your partner for life. If you find his or her tastes, preferences, habits, attitudes, character, personality perfectly in sync with yours, become worried—the other person is either faking it to win you over or is a twin your parents lost at the Kumbh Mela.

Chances are that some qualities will be in sync, some will not and some you will spend a lifetime discovering—men live in the head, women are more emotional, intuitive and live in the heart, but as long as there are no major disparities, it looks like a match well made. Besides, if you are exactly like each other, there will be nothing to learn and nothing to discover and very little to talk about. On the other hand, if there are many differences, you might find yourself with more to learn than you can handle. Ask each other questions, consult your parents or whoever you trust and respect before deciding to take the plunge. It's a delicate balancing act and you have to go about it wisely.

FULFILLING THE MARRIAGE DHARMA

In India, marriage has always been considered a sacred bond, made in heaven, between two souls. As the institution of marriage finds itself under assault from the stresses of modern life, perhaps this is a good time to take a fresh look at the lessons ancient India has to offer us.

The most important ritual in a Hindu wedding is the saptapadi or the seven sacred vows. Each vow is a promise that the couple make to each other:

1. To respect and honour each other.
2. To share each other's joys and sorrows.
3. To trust and be loyal to each other.
4. To cultivate appreciation for knowledge, values, sacrifice and service.
5. To appreciate purity of emotions, love, family duties and spiritual growth.
6. To follow the principles of dharma.
7. To nurture an eternal bond of friendship and love.

Similar to the saat phere or the saptapadi ritual is the mangal phera, which consists of the couple taking four circles or 'pheras' around the fire. Either ritual is performed based on the variations of the ceremony. While the saptapadi is more common and also noticeably relevant, mangal phera is frequently used to highlight the four basic goals of life. Each of these four cycles represents a promise just as each phera does in the saptapadi ritual. The couple begins their walk around the fire, each completed circle representing the four stages of life:

1. To pursue life's religious and moral duty (dharma).
2. To pursue prosperity (artha).
3. To pursue earthly pleasures (kama).
4. To pursue spiritual salvation (moksha).

RELEVANCE OF A FEW IMPORTANT WEDDING RITUALS

Indian culture is unique, unparalleled and full of good attributes and features. Every philosophy, every rite and ritual, every thought and action is designed for the evolution and betterment of the human being. There is no custom in India that is not imbued with a special significance. In fact, behind most of them lies a deeper, scientific meaning.

The wedding rites too have been designed keeping all these factors in mind. Threaded into a wedding ceremony, the rituals with their rightful importance assume prime significance in the union. A few of these are explained below:

The mehendi (henna) applied a day or two before the actual wedding has not only a cosmetic appeal but also medicinal benefits. Applied on the hands and feet of the bride, which have many nerve endings, mehendi helps to prevent the nerves from becoming tense during stressful situations.

The traditional haldi (turmeric) ceremony involves applying turmeric paste to the groom and bride on the big day. Apart from imparting a natural glow, this medicinal herb helps to keep bacteria at bay. Prepared with oil, this gold concoction helps to moisturize the skin as well.

The holy fire around which the couple takes their vows also has its own scientific significance. The fire, which is ignited using sandalwood and ghee, is topped with other satvik products like rice and herbal ingredients too. Smoke emitting from it purifies the surrounding environment with positivity.

The sindoor which the groom applies on his bride's forehead is also meant to reduce stress.

The toe rings worn by married women in India also sit tight with valid scientific justification. They strengthen the uterus as a nerve from the second toe on which the ring is worn connects the uterus and passes through the heart. This helps to regularize the menstrual cycle and keeps the reproductive organ healthy.

Bangles are integral to any bride's attire. They not only add colour and a jingling sound, but also help to improve blood circulation and activate acupressure points for good health.

The bindi hits the nail on the head as it is the spot where major nerves of the body meet. Massaging this point, in the process of applying it often, helps in relieving headaches.

If Avi and Kavya had listened closely to the pujari (priest) who presided over the sacred fire that burns at wedding ceremonies, perhaps they would have learnt to read more into the various mantras and rituals that have now been reduced to rituals that are performed perfunctorily. The vows can be connected to the philosophy of yoga or the spiritual teachings of India, which offer prescriptions for happiness in all walks of life.

Marriage calls for commitment. Here's the maths: For the sake of convenience, let's take an arbitrary figure—suppose there are twenty years of togetherness in an average Indian marriage. That's 7,300 days, which is 1,75,200 hours—more than enough time to melt a tonne of ice cream in Antarctica. Those signing up should keep this in mind. Asmarohana, one of the many Hindu wedding rituals, requires the couple to step on a grinding stone which is symbolic of the firmness in the commitment to marriage and the determination to overcome conflicts and challenges.

In the good old days, the pace of change was slow, and twenty years lasted for twenty years, sometimes longer. But change is rapid now—the whole world around is in constant motion and you can change your immediate environment at the flick of a button on the remote control. But they have not yet made a remote control that will make Avi sulk less or Kavya less possessive; therefore, commitment does not come easily to this generation, and that perhaps makes it even more important. Regular practice of the yoga way of living would have helped Avi and Kavya to overcome their misunderstandings and make them aware of their true dharma. Adharma is also manifested in personal grudges, likes and dislikes, hatred, envy, jealousy and greed. This is entirely opposite to dharma and results in stress, illness, chaos, cacophony, conflicts and confusion. Both the mind and body become afflicted.

'Dharma' is a word used often in the context of spirituality; a most desirable virtue, it means 'a sense of duty' or 'doing the right thing'. It is said that there would be more peace in the world if everybody did his duty, and just as it is the dharma of a teacher to teach well, it is the dharma of a spouse to stay committed in the face of all odds. Of course, the commitment gets rewarded, but more about that later.

Accepting challenges goes hand in hand with commitment. Does this sound like you are being prepared for war? Actually, you are. But it need not be combative—both parties can sit at the table and negotiate a win-win deal for both. Both can win this war. That calls for patience, communication, clear thinking. Commitment is good for fixing a car that is stationary, accepting challenges requires you to get on top of the car when it is running and fix it; there will be surprises and challenges coming up at frequent intervals, so keep your spanners and strategies handy, and you will benefit, as the following story illustrates.

A couple was celebrating their golden anniversary, and on being asked about their strategy for a long happy married life, it emerged that soon after their marriage they made a pact with each other. As both were short-tempered, they decided to follow a strategy when one of them lost his/her temper. The woman requested, 'When I get angry, I do not want you near me, I do not want to see you, so please go out for a walk.' The man agreed and in turn requested, 'When I get angry, please don't say anything, please just be quiet for some time and, later, I will buy you anything you want!' The pact was signed, and it worked well for both of them. Frequent walks kept the man healthy and the woman could tick off a lot of items on

Practising Yoga for a Happy Married Life ▶▶ 21

her shopping list. And what happened to the issues that got them angry in the first place?

Time has the ability to shrink even major issues into insignificant matters, and they knew that if they succeeded in dodging the first few minutes after the explosion, the fire would die down, and more often than not, it did. To be angry is to let others' mistakes punish you, the Buddha said. If the couple had confronted each other instead of dodging, they would have started, like most couples do, pulling out past hurts and aches from their collective memory: 'You said this to me last year,' 'Your parents did not buy me a gift five years ago,' and so on. Not only did they learn to strategize to benefit each other, their relationship grew stronger when they learnt that it was possible to deal skilfully with a situation and manage it instead of being overwhelmed by it. It gave them pride and the confidence that they could handle the challenges life would throw at them. It taught them to solve their problems creatively and it also taught them patience. Strategy is important and it should be a win-win situation for all.

Saloni pulls out three saris from her cupboard—she loves all of them—and asks her husband, Bob, to help her pick one for the evening's party. Saloni gets to wear one of her three favourites and her husband is happy that he was consulted. Everybody's happy. That's a win-win strategy. Avi and Kavya could have learnt a trick or two from this couple; a clever person learns from his mistakes, a cleverer person learns from his own as well as other people's mistakes.

To see another's viewpoint, a person with a size ten shoe should try walking a few hundred metres in a shoe of a smaller size. Literally—only to understand that there is another point of view. The story of a Chinese student illustrates this well.

Chan was studying in the US. One day the dean of his college decided to make the rounds of the college and meet students. He spoke cordially to all of them and inquired about their well-being. Soon it was Chan's turn to shake hands with the dean. On being asked what he thought about his fellow American students, Chan said, 'Oh, they are all very nice, but there's one thing I just can't get over.' And when Chan was asked what that one thing was, he said, 'They have funny eyes,' he replied. That day the dean learnt that it was not only the Chinese who had 'funny' eyes; the Americans had them too, and maybe everyone has them, depending on the perspective of those looking at them. There is always another point of view, and acknowledging this fact teaches you to respect others as well as yourself.

According to a folktale, being born a human is a gift and, for the moment, let's disregard the staggering population numbers. The tale goes like this: a tortoise lives at the bottom of the ocean (no one knows which one), and at some point it swims up to the surface and sticks its head out. A man standing in a boat in the ocean tosses a ring into the ocean in the hope that it will fall around the tortoise's neck although he has no idea if the tortoise lives in that ocean. The chances of that happening are the same as the chances of being born a human being, according to the tale. The occurrence then of two humans finding each other and deciding to come together in this vast ocean of life to seek love and compatibility, if looked at with the awe and respect it deserves, will automatically draw forth the commitment it requires.

It is said that a family person is equal to a thousand sanyasis. If, as is believed in India, the purpose of life is self-realization, that is, learning acceptance and selflessness, overcoming the ego, developing a broader vision and a wider perspective, then marriage is indeed a crash course. The sanyasi waits for life to throw lessons at him in order to learn from them; the householder has a home tutor. Two people together can make twice as many mistakes, but if one looks at the upside, two people together with a healthy dose of patience and a poor dose of ego can learn twice as fast from each other's mistakes.

You are what you do, you are what you think, you are also what you eat. For example, a person who eats spicy food is more likely to lose his temper easily than one who eats sattvic (light) food.

FOUR PILLARS FOR A HAPPY LIFE

Yoga stresses the importance of the following four pillars for a happy life:

AHAR (FOOD)

Ahar is the kind of food you eat. What and how you eat also matters; for example, eating your meals while watching TV doesn't allow you to enjoy the taste of the food and also hampers your digestion. As described earlier, a sattvic diet is a pure vegetarian diet, which includes seasonal fresh fruits, fresh vegetables, whole grain, pulses, sprouts, dried nuts, seeds, honey, fresh herbs, milk and dairy products. These foods raise sattva or the consciousness levels. A rajasic diet mainly consists of foods which contain spices and richness in taste, such as onions and garlic, deep-fried food, coffee, tea, refined food items, sugary food and chocolates. These foods give instant energy for a brief period, but ultimately, we get to experience low energy levels or stress. A tamasic diet chiefly consists of reheated foods, chemically processed foods, eggs, meat and alcohol. These foods will make the person dull, unimaginative, unmotivated, careless and lethargic.

VIHAR (RECREATION)

Me-time is important. Your first dharma is towards yourself. If you are not happy, you will not be able to make others happy. Niyamas can cut out the chaos and bring about order in your lives.

ACHAR (CONDUCT)

Achar relates to your conduct. It is about cultivating the right habits, attitude and code of conduct to improve your lifestyle. Since each individual is unique, you have to take extreme care of how you deal with the other. Your conduct with others should be loving, caring and cordial at all times. A certain amount of routine and discipline will bring order in your life. Incorporating an exercise routine, for example, in your daily schedule can guarantee good health. Eating, sleeping and waking up at the right time will enable you to function smoothly.

VICHAR (THOUGHTS)

Your thoughts build your character, your reality and your life. You have to be aware of your thinking pattern and focus on managing your thought process. It is in fact the first and foremost lesson in the yoga way of life. There is increasing evidence now that the mind affects the body; a disturbed mind and consequent psychosomatic illnesses can be kept at bay by cultivating a balanced outlook. Observing the yamas and niyamas can aid in this process.

3

LEARNING ACCEPTANCE THROUGH YOGA

Ranbir and Radhika had been married for a few months when something started bugging Ranbir. While he was particular about time, Radhika was slower than the hour-arm on the clock. She was always late and then when she did get out of her state of slumber, she was always dashing around to get things done. If they had to go out for dinner, Radhika could be counted on to be late for breakfast the next day. Ranbir overlooked this behaviour as he was certain that Radhika would change after marriage. But the only thing that changed was Ranbir's blood pressure; it went high every time she showed up late. How long would he have to tolerate this, he fumed regularly. He wanted her to change but that's easier said than done.

If Ranbir had looked at the situation from Radhika's point of view, he would have been surprised. She was brought up in a different environment—her parents were artists and they worked at their own pace—according to her, only newspaper delivery boys and milkmen rose early! She believed that Ranbir suffered from anxiety and needed to learn to relax. To a certain extent, she was right. Actually, both needed to learn things from each other, and this learning can happen only after mutual acceptance. Acceptance that the cards have been dealt and everyone has to play the best game possible with their own set of cards. Unlike consumer products that can be returned on Amazon and Flipkart, a 'defective' spouse cannot be returned. Acceptance has to be total. At the conclusion of the Hindu wedding ceremony, there is a ritual called dhruvadarshan. The priest directs the newly-weds' eyes to the pole star, which remains steadfast in the sky though the stars around it move across the sky; this is meant to symbolize the steadfastness of their bond despite distractions. The tying of a knot with the ends of the groom's and the bride's garments at the wedding ceremony also symbolizes the eternal nature of the relationship.

As the song 'Boxer' goes, 'After changes upon changes, we're more or less the same.' This could be said about relationships too. The more you try to change your partner, the greater the resistance you will face. In fact, at one level, we are like children. If you tell a child to refrain from eating chocolate, you have already aroused his curiosity, and he will definitely eat one; if his parent finds out about it and makes a big issue, then the chocolate becomes even more important. The child reasons that the chocolate is desirable not just because it tastes good, but eating it also becomes an act of defiance; he wants to let his parents know that he is a person with a mind of his own, so he goes ahead and has some more chocolate. Even if Radhika did realize the virtues of waking up early and being on time, her ego would remind her that if she became punctual as Ranbir desired then she would become a puppet in the hands of her husband. To keep her pride intact and her ego propped up, she probably remained unpunctual to prove a point. According to a Chinese saying, 'It is easier to reshape a river or a mountain than a person.'

If Ranbir stopped nagging her, then she only had her own conscience to battle, and conscience will eventually win over ego. Nagging, which might seem like an effective strategy to bring about change, only delays the inevitable. Attitude matters a lot. Tired of nagging, Ranbir decided that he would use the time before Radhika woke up to catch up on his reading, and since he enjoyed sipping his morning cup of tea with his wife, he decided he would wait until she woke up and joined him for tea. He decided to put his expectations aside and accept the situation instead. And how did this happen? One day when Radhika told him that she would start waking up early if he would just wake up ten minutes later, he did exactly that. At first, it was almost impossible; the alarm clock in his body would not allow him to wake up late. He became aware of the tight grip of habit, realizing that it would take him long to change a small habit. That is when he decided to accept Radhika the way she was. Barring extreme situations, acceptance is an absolute must. As Dr Mahesh Parikh, a psychiatrist associated with The Yoga Institute, says, 'One cannot be happy in marriage unless one is divorced—divorced from one's own notions, beliefs, views. We have to rid ourselves of the coloured glasses we wear and view the world for what it truly is.'

ACCEPTANCE THROUGH YOGA

Yoga helps you realize that everything is impermanent, so the opinion you have today may not be relevant tomorrow, or the person next to you may not be around tomorrow. Opinions, situations, solutions, likes and dislikes keep changing. Then why do we remain attached to everything and everyone?

All of it stems from avidya, which is ignorance or lack of the right knowledge. In the *Yoga Sutras*, Patanjali says that ignorance lies in regarding the impermanent as permanent, the impure as pure, the painful as pleasant and the non-self as the self.

All that which is impermanent (anitya), you believe to be permanent (nitya). Your body, relations, thoughts, your whole life is not permanent. Everything is changing. But we live as if everything is permanent.

All that is impure (asuchi) is considered to be pure (suchi). The body is not pure, and beauty is skin-deep. When you wash your hands you believe them to be clean but they are home to so many germs and bacteria. Also, many a time a person's thoughts are impure and yet, just because he sports a fake smile, his thoughts and intentions are believed to be pure.

Anything that you think will give you happiness (sukha), will ultimately give you unhappiness (dukha) and misery. All that gives you pleasure at one time will actually be painful for you in the long run. In the Mahabharata, we have seen how Duryodhana showed extreme pleasure when Draupadi was dragged by her hair in the court to be disrobed. In that moment, he didn't realize that his act would bring down his entire existence.

Your body is not yours, your mind also is not yours—it does not behave as you want it to. Even your children, your business, or anything else is not completely yours. What is yours is only your consciousness, but it's not easy to reach that level of realization.

Therefore, you should not get attached to anybody or anything. Never nurse your ego by convincing yourself that you are superior. Only do your duty and live in the moment.

CHANGE YOURSELF TO CHANGE OTHERS

These days one hears about many marriages breaking up in a short time, and one often hears that so-and-so, after his or her divorce, is now very happy with the new spouse. What happened? Did the fates suddenly decide one day that X, whose wife left him because he is a perfect rascal, deserves a better spouse like Y because he deserves happiness? Not really. Chances are that X, chastened by his experience, decided that he would bring about some of the changes his ex-wife wanted him to for the sake of better compatibility in future. How do you make a vertical line longer without touching it? By drawing a smaller line next to it. X decided to become bigger than his expectations, than his ego; if he had brought about these changes earlier, the break-up could have been avoided. But as Dr Jayadeva once said, 'God gives us a comb only after we have lost all our hair.'

Nothing prepares a young couple for the challenges that lie ahead. If they could be counselled about the future, about the need to prepare oneself, if they were informed that the real world will begin one day and that the honeymoon period will end, people would be aware of the fact that happiness is not given but has to be worked at. Couples who are about to get married should seek premarital counselling to equip them for the future because in India, and probably many other places too, a marriage is not just between two people but between families as well, and when dark clouds start to hover over a relationship, more than two people are affected.

Ranbir also figured out another way to win Radhika over. One evening, they were invited for dinner at a friend's place. While Ranbir made his way to the party straight from the office, Radhika strolled in an hour later. Their friends, used to seeing Ranbir peeved at Radhika's late arrivals, were expecting to be amused by Ranbir's sulking. But Ranbir had learnt a few things—Radhika was an artist, her temperament was different, and Ranbir had learnt to appreciate the fact that his wife was unable to tear herself away easily when she was in the middle of a painting. The downside was that she was late, the upside was there was a beautiful painting in progress. Ranbir greeted her warmly and announced to the others that her late-coming meant a great work of art was coming up, and he was, therefore, not upset at all. Radhika was moved by Ranbir's words and she decided that she would henceforth show up in time if only to make Ranbir happy. Ranbir finally got what he wanted when he stopped looking for it. At the next meeting with friends, he was happy to see her waiting for him instead.

Your attitude, your point of view matters a lot. You spend a lot of your time dodging challenges, trying to escape upheavals, and it's only natural. But just as you can't build muscles by watching others working out, you can build your emotional, intellectual and spiritual muscles only by facing challenges. You must decide for yourself how far you wish to be challenged and try to step out of your own comfort zone; a loose guitar string makes no music and an overstretched guitar string breaks, but a finely strung guitar string with just the right amount of tension is the only one capable of making music. Growth can only take place where there are challenges; a balanced outlook accelerates the pace of learning. The following story about two brothers illustrates this point well. One of the boys grew up to be a lazy, depressed alcoholic, the other one was always positive, worked at his job with enthusiasm and had a steady income. On being asked, the first one blamed his alcoholic father, believing that that is how he had ended up becoming an alcoholic himself. The other brother said he was what he was because his father was an alcoholic; he had seen his father ruin his own life and his family's. Instead of trying to change his father, which seemed impossible, he had sworn that he would never become like him and he decided to move on. In fact, when the father saw that his son was looking after him as he grew old and unwell, he decided that he would try to mend his ways. This story shows two people in the same situation with two different responses. Your attitude and your outlook shape you.

LAW OF KARMA AND MARRIAGE

In India, people believe in the law of karma. Perhaps some people take it too far and use the law of karma to justify their own faults, their laziness, and their lack of interest in taking charge of their own lives. According to the law of karma, one is born (not necessarily stuck) with certain qualities, and it is also said that it is karma that brings two people together in a marital bond. This way of looking at marriage suggests that two people will continue to meet each other in birth after birth until they make peace with each other. Some will call this a fatalistic attitude, but one has to contend with the fact that some things, however hard one tries, are beyond one's control. Even those who don't subscribe to this 'karma' view would do well to appreciate the fact that their lives will touch each other in significant ways and you owe it to the other person to recognize his or her humanity and to be sensitive and responsive to his or her needs, to do unto others as we would have them do unto us.

Most people get married believing that it is an opportunity to influence and change their partner's thinking and behaviour. If people entered it believing instead that this could be a good opportunity to learn about and better oneself, more marriages would be successful. After all, it is the ability to re-engineer one's own self that separates humans from animals. Only a human being aspires, if at all, to be a better human being. You will never hear a cat saying it wants to be a better cat.

ANITYA BHAVNA

Anitya Bhavna is a very simple mental exercise to broaden one's vision and learn acceptance.

1. Sit down in a quiet corner in a comfortable position. Most people find sitting with the back against the wall with their legs stretched out in front of them and their

hands on their thighs with their palms facing up fairly comfortable, but don't be rigid about this.
2. Close your eyes.
3. Repeat the following words in your mind or record them in your phone and play them back to yourself:
What was there in the morning is not there in the evening, what was there in the evening is not there in the night.
What was there yesterday is not there today, what was there today will not be there tomorrow.
Why should I then worry myself about something that is temporary and will pass away soon?
4. Repeat it a few times, reflect upon it and internalize it.
This meditation exercise is practised by many of our students at The Yoga Institute and it has benefitted them immensely.

4

BUILDING TRUST THROUGH YOGA

Geeta and Ajay had been happily married for twenty-five years. As they approached their middle age, Geeta started having some health problems and this often resulted in mood swings. On investigation, it was diagnosed that her health issues and her mood swings were a result of her menopause. This started to create problems at home. Fearing the passing away of her youth, Geeta started losing her self-confidence, which further turned her into a suspicious and overbearing person. She started doubting Ajay's integrity, accusing him of lacking commitment to their marriage. If she so much as found Ajay speaking to one of their female friends, she would fly into a rage, making all sorts of allegations. On a few occasions, she even threatened to walk out of the house. It was a difficult situation at home.

In the film *Lage Raho Munna Bhai*, Sanjay Dutt's recurring visions of Mahatma Gandhi were attributed to a 'chemical locha' by a psychiatrist, that is, a chemical imbalance. In Geeta's case too, one could trace her mood swings to hormonal changes caused by menopause. By constantly projecting her own insecurities about her marriage, Geeta was destroying a happy twenty-five-year-old union. But it's not always a chemical locha that upsets the apple cart of trust, which is, as we all know, a most vital ingredient in a happy marriage.

The inability to trust another is intrinsic to humans, and it is perhaps a good thing. It is a defence mechanism, essential for survival, and if you do not have this inbuilt defence mechanism, you would go through life trusting everyone blindly and, consequently, getting hurt and exploited. A lot of people do; the gullible, the innocent, the naïve go through life with blind faith in people, institutions, gurus, politicians and others until they learn that the ability to discern, that is, viveka (right understanding) in yoga terms, would serve them better in life. The ability to differentiate between the real and unreal, eternal and temporary, takes time. You have, knowingly or unknowingly, invested time in futile relationships and now you know better. Trust then is a function of time.

When two people get married in an arranged marriage set-up, they are almost strangers to each other. This is particularly true of India, where arranged marriages are common. In the case of love marriage, the partners have known each other for some time, but the tug of love and hormones, a potent mix, deludes them into believing that they know each other very well and forever—*janam-janam ka saath*, as they say in the movies. Often, reality dawns in some time and a partner realizes that the person he or she is married to is different from one they were courting. Friction, flare-ups follow and the marriage is over before it started. What went wrong? What has gone wrong with the present-day society? The entire world over, we are witnessing marriages that fizzle out easily, couples part, and both parties are left with a lot of pain and emotional scars. Why was it different in the so-called good old days? Why were marriages more enduring?

One of the many reasons for this could be the fact that people lived in smaller communities, smaller towns, and almost everyone knew each other. As everyone knew everyone, when one went out husband- or wife-hunting, most often than not, one knew what one was getting into. The city, on the other hand, with its millions of people from vastly different backgrounds guarantees anonymity to everyone and throws total strangers into proximity. One chooses one's partner from this vast swirling mix of humans, which is often akin to playing roulette at a gambling table, and, therefore, is it any surprise that divorce rates are soaring?

But this is reality and you can only learn to make the best of it. As mentioned earlier, trust is a function of time, and men and women who are planning to take the plunge should spend as much time with each other and each other's family as they can. A teacher of a spiritual sect advises his followers to 'study the product well before investing in it'. He likens the process to the purchase of a pot. 'When we go looking for a pot for our house, we tap various pots, pick them up, feel them, look into its insides,' he advises, 'before putting our money down, and every one of us should be doing this before signing up with a spiritual teacher.' The same advice could be extended to signing up for a long-term relationship like marriage if one wishes to have at least a minimum amount of trust before setting sail. Of course, this is not foolproof. As you would know from experience, the only way to find out if you can trust a person is to decide to do so. (After checking his/her Facebook page, of course.)

Once the ship of marriage sets sailing, the seas are rough at times, and, often, one is tossed around because one starts out as a novice sailor who has yet to learn the art of negotiating high waters. Lack of trust in each other is often the result of:

Building Trust through Yoga ▸▸ 37

1. Low self-esteem and a lack of trust in oneself.
2. Lack of empathy.
3. Poor interpersonal communication skills.

All the above are sometimes compounded by the new monster unleashed upon us called WhatsApp. So when Anika, just one year into her marriage, received a WhatsApp message from her husband, Neel, which read, 'Back late. Senior manager from Delhi visiting, insists she wants to go out for dinner', her low self-esteem teamed up with her fertile imagination and insecurities dragged her, as she hung by her fingertips to her sanity, on a crazy rollercoaster ride.

This is what she could have been thinking (vis-à-vis the above mentioned points).

1. 'Just one year into our marriage and he's not even bothered to call me to inform me. He's just sent a hurried WhatsApp message. Why? Is he up to mischief? Is he worried that I will sense the guilt in his voice and catch him out? I wonder what she looks like. Am I not attractive? Is the magic of marriage wearing off for him?' Other thoughts along similar lines must have flooded her mind, making her restless, unhappy and even angry. Worse, she was between jobs, and she had nothing to do, so her idle mind turned into a devil's workshop. Low self-esteem is what it was.
2. Lack of empathy: Anika could have for a moment considered the possibility that maybe he was busy at work, he had a deadline to meet and was therefore, unable to call, or maybe he was in a meeting and was unable to call, or maybe he was worried his friends would tease him for being a *'joru ka ghulam*

(henpecked)' if they learnt he was calling her often.
3. A perfectly innocuous message sent through WhatsApp can seem very offensive if not worded carefully. 'Back late' sounds cold compared to 'Back late, honey' accompanied by a smiley. Of course, we are often insensitive in our face-to-face communication as well, and misunderstandings are caused through other media too.

Anika was perhaps justified in the way she felt. You need to know that people close to you are sensitive about the way you treat them and speak to them—many of us get hurt easily, all of us have active imaginations; all these factors should be kept in mind. You need to stretch yourself a bit, even go out of your way to reassure others, particularly those who are close to you. Perhaps you also need to stretch yourself a bit in order to trust others. In the words of Frank Crane, 'You may be miserable if you trust too much, but you will be worse off if you don't trust enough.'

If Neel had taken a little trouble and called, Anika would have felt fine. If he had told her that if he was unable to call in future due to an urgent meeting, she should not take it amiss, she would have been better prepared. If he had taken an extra second to add a smiling emoji to his message, she would have felt better. If Neel had some more self-esteem, he would not have worried about his friends teasing him and would have called Anika anyway. If, instead of fretting and keeping all her feelings bottled up inside her, Anika had just jokingly asked him 'How old is your senior manager?' she would have learnt that she was sixty-two and, well, no competition at all. Communication and transparency are key to building trust.

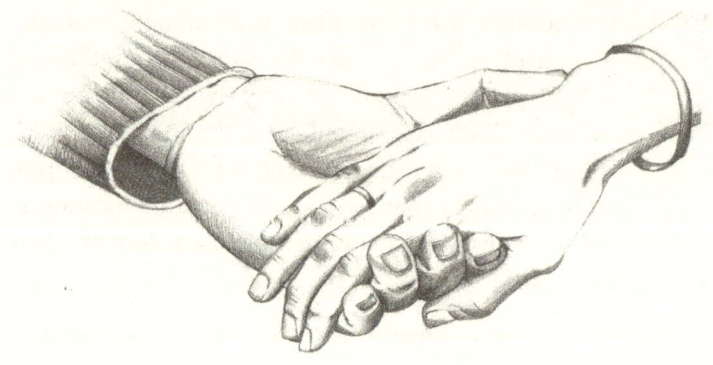

Communication is the key, but one also doesn't have to go to the other extreme. There is no need to unload details of your past life, names of your ex-girlfriends and ex-boyfriends on each other once you are in a committed relationship. It's best to leave the past behind and keep moving ahead. Digging up the past is not a sign of honesty, but a sign of stupidity.

It is clearly established that in order to develop trust in marriage, one has to work on oneself. Many people lack self-esteem, and the world hammers one into believing that one is an ordinary mortal—often, those who have self-esteem have more than their share, bordering on arrogance. A spiritual education is essential to help you build faith in yourself, to look at your own self in a positive manner, to respect yourself without becoming vain. When you are able to know and trust yourself, it becomes possible to learn to trust others too; otherwise, you remain a victim of your own fears and suspicions. A spiritual education also teaches you some amount of detachment and self-reliance, again essential qualities that can replace dependence with interdependence. Trust comes easily to the strong. A conscious effort has to be made to strengthen the muscle of trust, and premarital counselling can help a lot in pointing the about-to-be-married towards the right direction.

Quite often, you know deep down in your heart if the person you have chosen to trust is trustworthy or not (unless, of course, this person is a very good actor). Sometimes you choose to fool yourself into believing that the person is trustworthy; you don't want to believe the worst about this person and so you lie to yourself. This dishonesty can prove to be expensive. 'Satya' (honesty), the second yama, doesn't require you to be honest only with others but also with yourself. If you could train your mind to put your own likes and prejudices aside, if you could train yourself to look at a person or a situation with objectivity and dispassion, you would probably find yourself facing the truth. Your body also sends you warning signals (that is why it is called 'gut feeling'). If you find yourself feeling uncomfortable in a person's presence, your body has picked up the cues before your uncertain, wavering mind can and is trying to tell you something. You have to learn to listen to your body too.

Time plays a vital part in building relationships and developing trust. Instead of pointing accusing fingers at the other, the question to ask yourself when you find your relationship tottering on a weak foundation of trust is: 'Did I do enough to win his or her trust?' You may be surprised to find that the answer lies within you.

GUT FEELING

The left brain is responsible for rational and analytical thinking. As one becomes increasingly 'logical' and 'rational', one tends to neglect one's right brain, which is responsible for intuition, creativity and thoughtfulness. Often, one has a certain feeling about a certain person, a prospective job or employer or a contract, and this gut feeling or 'inner voice' warns one to steer clear and not trust this entity. 'Gut feeling' is a psychosomatic phenomenon and it is so called because the intestines house the enteric nervous system, sometimes called the 'second brain'. Hence, it could be your second brain warning you. Should you be listening to this inner voice? It could be right, it could be your intuition warning you. It could also be wrong because it could be an irrational fear. Sometimes one overthinks and overanalyses and takes the wrong decision, sometimes one doesn't analyse enough and takes the wrong decision. How can you learn to distinguish between gut feelings and irrational fears? Here are two ways:

1. Intuition is about the present; there is no worrying about the past or future.
2. Gut feeling is neutral whereas irrational fears are charged with emotion.

Listening to one's intuition or one's heart, learning to trust one's gut feeling is worth learning and gets better with practice.

Yoga teaches you to keep calm and not get swayed by emotions, and this practice of '*chitta vritti nirodha*' (Sutra 1.2, *Yoga Sutras* of Patanjali), that is, stilling the mind or removing the fluctuations of the mind is the essence of yoga. When the mind is calm and relaxed, it's possible to see clearly.

CONDITIONING

The practice of conditioning is primarily practised to gather thoughts and calm the mind. At The Yoga Institute, the meditative posture, Sukhasana, is instrumental to 'condition' the mind. Conditioning is to stop the chatter and attract the mind inwards. It also helps in 'restructuring' the mind. This practice also readies the mind for further practice of asanas, pranayamas and kriyas. It can be also practised independently to calm and steady the mind.

The practice of conditioning can be done by anyone.

METHOD OF PRACTICE

Preferably sit in Sukhasana or on a straight-backed chair. Take care to keep your back erect. Check that you are not slouching. Keep your head straight, elbows and shoulders relaxed, palms facing down, resting on your thighs or knees.

Watch your breath for about ten to fifteen minutes. Try not to let your mind wander. However, in case it does, bring it back by watching your breath without getting disturbed.

This practice greatly aids in bringing a distracted mind to attentiveness and aids concentration. It reduces extraneous thoughts and makes one mindful, encouraging being in the present. It also brings clarity of thought and an inner harmony arises as there is less nervous agitation.

NISHPANDA BHAVA

Nishpanda bhava is one of the most powerful techniques developed by the founder of The Yoga Institute. You traverse through life holding on to all and sundry, from your material possessions to your thoughts, opinions, likes, dislikes, grudges, regrets and insatiable desires.

This simple technique teaches you that life goes by just like the sounds around you. These sounds represent life, its events, situations and people who come and go. You need to understand that they persist, acknowledge them and allow yourself to move on without regret, analysis and judgement.

METHOD OF PRACTICE

Sit on a mat leaning against a wall with feet apart and outstretched. Do not slouch. Let the hips be close to the wall so that the spine remains naturally erect. The hands rest on the thighs, the palms and fingers are loose and facing upwards.

Close your eyes and passively observe the passing sounds as they come and fade away. Do not dwell on any sound but let it go as it fades away. Pick up on the next sound in the surrounding atmosphere.

If there are no sounds, you can then focus on some light instrumental music but no words as words tend to develop emotions and reactions in the mind.

Do not get affected by any sound in any way.

Sit in this manner for 5 to 15 minutes.

This technique, when understood and practised in its true

spirit elevates us from the mundane to the extraordinary. It is excellent to develop 'vairagya bhava'. It creates a feeling of 'body forgetfulness' which helps the body to heal faster. It is also recommended in every sickness of body and mind and otherwise.

5

COMMUNICATING EFFECTIVELY THROUGH PRANAYAMA

Robin and Aditi had an arranged marriage. Aditi believed she was lucky to have found Robin who was handsome, highly qualified, with a good job and was from a well-established family. In the first few years of marriage, Aditi was in seventh heaven. As time passed, they started discovering each other's differences, and Aditi found that while she enjoyed talking to people, Robin was quite the opposite. Given a chance, he would speak in monosyllables. When he returned from his workplace, she would be eager to share the day's happenings with him, but Robin would respond with a mere grunt or a nod. The newspaper seemed more important to him; the events unfolding between Donald Trump and Kim Jong were more interesting for him than the exotic new recipes she had learnt especially for him. This was the beginning of some serious communication problems between them, with Aditi accusing him of not paying enough attention to her and not being concerned about her well-being. Harsh words were exchanged at times, resulting in the ruffling of feathers of both parties. Obviously, words are potent weapons, capable of great harm, more than we may understand them to be.

An example of the power of words is illustrated by this story: A young spiritual aspirant met a teacher and requested him to show him the way to higher learning and self-realization. The teacher obliged him and told him to repeat the mantra 'I am' over a hundred times a day. The student was not very pleased with what he believed was a peculiar response on the teacher's part. 'What good will the repetition of these two words do to me? After all, they are mere words...' he complained. 'Okay,' the teacher said, 'if I had known you were such an idiot, I would not have wasted my time on you. The young man was stung by this answer. He flew into a rage and shouted, 'How dare you call me an idiot? How dare you?' 'Idiot, idiot, idiot,' the teacher repeated, 'that is what you are.' This angered the student even further, until he was on the verge of exploding. The teacher smiled at the student. 'That is the power of the word,' he told him. 'All I said was "idiot" and it had you fuming and frothing; similarly, the use of the right words can take a person to great heights.' The student begged for forgiveness—he had learnt his lesson.

Words matter, how they are uttered matters. Call a person a fool and he will blow his top. Put your arm around him and tell him gently to stop being a fool and you will have him eating out of your hand. Calling him a fool is bad communication, and putting your arm around him is good communication. Same message, different effect.

Most of us like to believe that we are experts in communication. We have a mouth, a tongue, we know a few words, and, well, that's good enough, isn't it? That's like a person saying, 'I have carrots, capsicum, peas, corn and now nothing can stop me from being a good chef.' A mouth and a tongue are merely the tools of communication, but an airplane needs an expert pilot to fly it. And God help those who have an inefficient pilot to steer their words; disasters and crashes are imminent.

Communication skills have to be learnt. Does it mean that we have to learn the right words, the right pronunciation, the correct accent? Behind the words lies the thought, and thought is in the domain of the mind. Yoga—and again, this is not to be confused with asanas—can teach us to steer our minds. After all, we communicate poorly only when we are confused, angry, upset, disturbed and agitated.

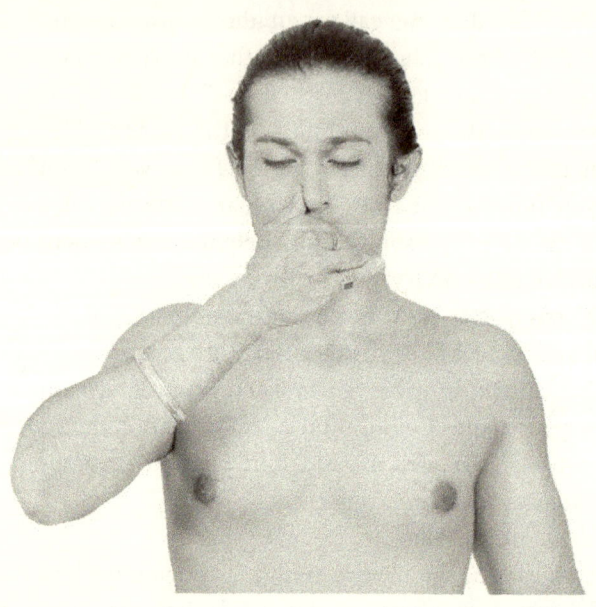

The yogic practice of pranayamas helps to manage the breath in such a way that the mind becomes steady and gets more clarity. While it is also advised to regularly observe one's normal breathing, pranayama aids in increasing concentration and promotes steadiness of mind and body. It also helps to balance and regulate emotions as well as reduces impulsive behaviour.

A sound body—in this case, read 'sound tongue'—requires a sound mind. How often have you said rude, hurtful things to others and then repented it? Sometimes you are at the receiving end too. To make sure this doesn't happen, a few guidelines are essential:

REFRAIN FROM SPEAKING WHEN YOU ARE IN A DISTURBED STATE OF MIND

When you find yourself in an unpleasant situation, the mind immediately starts to jump like a monkey and whip the creator of this situation with the tongue. It is difficult to restrain your tongue at this time. A slight from your spouse, or even a perceived slight, and you are ready to march to the battlefield. The following story illustrates the inability to control one's tongue: Three spiritual seekers had decided that they would accelerate their journey to self-realization by keeping quiet for two whole years, regardless of the circumstances. After a month in the woods, they saw a hare run past them into a grove. Tempted to comment on the hare yet determined to keep quiet, they kept their lips sealed. But, finally, after three months, one of them could not restrain himself, and he said, 'Did you see that beautiful white rabbit?' His friends glared at him for breaking the vow and kept quiet. Seeker number two appeared restless. He wanted to say something, and, finally, he did speak after seven months of silence. 'It was not white, it was grey,' he said. All of them were naturally upset by their own lack of restraint, but they kept quiet. Finally, unable to control himself, seeker number three spoke up after another eight months. 'Will you guys stop arguing?' he said.

The tongue, or actually the mind, is a tough one to rein in, underlying the importance of keeping calm while dealing with contentious issues.

SPEAK ONLY IF THE OTHER PERSON IS IN A RECEPTIVE MOOD

A man talked a lot in his sleep and also snored loudly. His wife was extremely disturbed by this double-noise nuisance. Together they visited a doctor to seek a remedy—and to the man's delight, the doctor's suggested cure was to allow the husband to speak more and also play some games during the day. The couple actually worked upon it and started sharing pleasant conversations, cracking jokes along with playing games like table tennis and carom. This change in their lifestyle routine helped build a better bonding and reduced the man's talking and snoring when he was sleeping.

If there's a burning issue at hand and you wish to talk about it to your spouse, it's best to wait for the right time. It is possible that your spouse has a work-related issue on his or her mind, or is trying to figure out which school to choose for the child or is busy skydiving. Sometimes it's better to make your point by writing it down.

CHECK IF THE MESSAGE HAS BEEN RECEIVED AS IT WAS INTENDED TO

The following joke illustrates this point. A woman leaves a note for her husband: 'I'll be back late tonight, so don't even think you can go out to the bar with your friends. Don't forget to call your mother, so she doesn't worry.' Men, it is said, have a talent for glossing over the details and reading or seeing only what they want to read or see. Glancing quickly over his wife's note, these are the words that stood out in her husband's eyes: 'Blah blah blah tonight blah blah you can go out to the bar with your friends. Don't blah blah blah worry.' So basically, he read: 'Tonight you can go out to the bar with your friends. Don't worry.'

Clearly, the message was not complied with, and was predictably followed by an explosive situation at home.

Mastering the rules of communication takes time and energy. A person who is agitated will more often than not shoot first and then eat his words later. A calm and relaxed state of mind is definitely more conducive for clear and effective communication, and it is a state of mind that has to be acquired with dogged effort. It may sound ridiculous because one throws words around so glibly that it is hard to believe that an act one takes so much for granted has to be learnt. But speaking is only one half of the deal; one learns to speak but no one talks about the importance of listening, which is equally important.

Today, many colleges and universities offer courses that teach interpersonal communication skills. Its significance is well understood by the corporate world, but its importance in our personal lives deserves equal importance. The ability to listen, to empathize, communicate diplomatically, with a problem-solving positive attitude, are qualities that are as essential at home and the workplace. They can help replace confrontations and arguments with collaboration and compromise.

Empathy is vital to communication too. In India, joint families are common, and a newly married woman moves into the household of her husband which includes parents, and in a an extended joint family, even uncles, aunts, cousins. Sometimes the more the merrier, but very often more is not merrier. The new bride is thrown into an environment which is a mix of people with varying temperaments, and keeping her balance can be challenging. Not being able to speak up openly about these situations with the one she is closest to, her husband, can be very stressful. Sometimes men find themselves in tricky situations. Men and women and their families have to learn to create an environment which encourages communication and transparency. Tact and diplomacy have to be learnt to carry out this tough balancing act.

In the case of Robin and Aditi, Robin will have to learn that Aditi, who has been looking forward all day to being with him when he returns from work, deserves much more than silence and grunts. Aditi, on the other hand, has to understand that maybe Robin had a rough day at work, maybe he needs to unwind before they can spend some quality time together.

HOW NOT TO COMMUNICATE

As you sow, so shall you reap. Everything you do, comes back to you. You have to be very alert about your karmas as you have to face the their consequences. Although karma means action, work or deed, according to yoga, you do karma in thoughts and words too. So the first rule is to see if your mind and thoughts are balanced and clear. Only then is it possible for you to communicate with clarity.

You also need to be mindful to understand if the person with whom you are communicating is also listening, which means that you must see if he is in a receptive state. If you follow this strictly, then the communication will not steer in the wrong direction. You need to maintain a good amount of faith (shraddha) and patience (saburi).

A lot can be learnt from the game Chinese Whispers.
Players needed: Four to six
Sit down in a circle. Whisper a completely innocuous

sentence, about eight to ten words long, very quickly, into the ear of the person next to you; the other players should not be able to hear it. The sentence could be something like, 'The brown cat there has a long white tail.'

The person next to you whispers it quickly into the ear of the person next to him. This goes on until the last person whispers it into your ear. Do not be surprised if what you finally hear is something like, 'The noun flat mare is wrong right pail.' What happened here was that everyone heard something other than what was said, and this is what happens in the real world too.

Learning from the game: All communication, whether it is between two or ten people, has to be clear, precise and conscious in order to convey what is meant to be conveyed. Hence, communicate carefully.

A word of caution: Do not believe in what you may listen from others. It is always best to communicate clearly and directly at the right time in the right manner.

6

DEVELOPING LOVE, INTIMACY THROUGH YOGA

Love. Books and poems have been written on the subject; almost all films must have a love story, heroes and heroines have chased each other sometimes even around trees, confessing their love for each other, publishing houses have made millions by publishing titles dedicated solely to love. Romeo and Juliet, Soni–Mahiwal, Heer–Ranjha, Laila–Majnu are only some of the many tales of enduring love that are now a part of our myths and folklore. Love turns ordinary men and women into poets and writers, philosophers and even warriors. In life and in our stories, people are either desperate to fall in love or have fallen prey to the pangs of love or are wondering how to get out of it. Some are willing to die for it, some are willing to kill for it. There may be variations on the theme of 'love' but the theme is centuries-old and there is little doubt that it will be there forever. And despite its permanent place in our lives, in our hearts and minds and our stories, it still confounds us. We still continue to ask, 'What is true love?'

Is there such a thing as true love? And if there is, then why does it fade away? The image of the young man who falls madly in love with someone and is later found drowning his sorrows in wine, the proverbial Devdas, is very common in our stories. Why do couples who professed to love each other till their dying days find themselves in marriage courts, ready to hurt and malign each other? How to make love last is a question that has concerned writers, thinkers, philosophers, psychologists and, of course, all those who fall in and out of love. They are still searching.

The dictionary definitions of love include 'A profound and caring affection towards someone' and 'A feeling of intense attraction towards someone'. It is on this 'attraction and affection' that most of us would like or would want to believe that our relationships, particularly marriage, are based on. In India though, there is a little spin on 'love'. In his book, *No Full Stops in India*, Mark Tully talks about meeting a village headman and their conversation on love and marriage. 'In England you marry the women you love. In India we love the women we marry,' the village headman is reported to have said. 'You fall out of love after marriage. We fall in love after marriage,' he added.

Cultural differences will always be there and the debate on 'arranged marriage' versus 'love marriage' can be endless. Both have advantages and disadvantages, both have successes and failures. In both cases, the parties concerned would be more than happy to have the genuine article, that is, love. Perhaps we can learn from both institutions. As modern life throws both sexes in close proximity, there is a likelihood that one could mistake the call of hormones for love; one could base one's relationship entirely on attraction. This is more often than not the basis of a short-term plan, and any relationship based solely on attraction and other similar superficial grounds is doomed from the beginning. Young people desirous of a lasting long-term relationship will need to introspect on whether it is love that beckons or just lust, which can blind and fool people by masquerading as love.

Like the doomed, short-term relationship based on lust, there are other equally self-destructive relationships founded on factors other than love.

Often, people can fool themselves into believing that they are in love with each other when, in fact, it is a selfish need-based relationship. If you are in a relationship to heal a wound or have a wound healed, then it's merely a need-based relationship. When the wound is healed, there may be nothing to bind the couple together. It's true that some relationships do grow beyond the immediate need, but one should be aware of the reason for the existence of the relationship. If one or both partners are there because one of them is diffident and needs the other to boost his or her self-esteem, or if one is nice to the partner's family, these are very thin grounds to base a lifelong commitment on. Often, the person doing the 'giving' gets tired of it but the taker doesn't tire of taking, and this creates a strain on the relationship. Or the person doing the taking may wake up to the fact that, for example, he or she needs a spouse for his or her own self and not for the family; this is bound to have hurtful consequences. All humans need attention and need to feel like they matter, but if one partner has this need to an unhealthy extreme, it could rock the boat.

Incomplete people tend to attract other incomplete people and are unable to complete and fulfil each other because both want to take from the relationship and have little to give. A healthy relationship in a case like this is not possible because the constant taking will eventually exhaust the parties concerned.

The important question then to ask yourself is: Am I in love or am I in need? If your answer is 'need', then there's trouble ahead. This can be better understood with an example.

Anusha had a lot of fears and insecurities. When she got married to Anand, she saw her husband as a source of security—physical, emotional and financial. She did little to confront her insecurities and they got in the way of her relationship; she was suspicious, paranoid and subsequently, started clinging to Anand, hovering over him, watching over him, and was always questioning him about his whereabouts and activities. Anand was patient initially but it finally got to him; he started to stay late at work because he wanted to avoid her, he spent more time with his friends, he used every excuse to get away from her and they continued to live unhappily ever after. It's a common enough theme, and often, it's the male who is the protagonist—the variations on this theme are endless.

Perhaps there is some truth in what the village headman told the writer about falling in love after marriage. While one cannot and should not rule out love marriage altogether, there is a possibility that the couple has mistaken the instant gratification of an immature relationship for love. Starting out on a peak, the only way the couple can head is down. On the other hand, the journey that begins at the foot of the hill, with little or no expectation, and is walked upon with commitment and resolve by two strong and mature individuals leads towards the peak, towards the goal called 'love'.

In nature, the givers always thrive; plants, trees, the earth, the sky give constantly and never tire of giving. It is ironical because it is understood that the taker will always have more and the giver will eventually give away everything and have nothing left, but nature appears to have turned it on its head. At the level of humans, it takes self-esteem, independence, strength, confidence to give to another and nurture a loving relationship.

Yoga teaches and encourages one to cultivate these virtues. The yamas and niyamas, if practised sincerely, can teach one to give more, to expect less, to strive, to introspect and reflect, to think clearly and act decisively. This is possible if one commits oneself to incorporate these values into one's life; it takes time but it can be done. Asanas work at the level of the body and the mind. If practised in earnest, yoga makes it possible to become a healthy, happy, positive, well-rounded individual and well-rounded individuals are better equipped to nurture healthy relationships. Love is visible in caring.

While on the subject of love, it is important to touch upon intimacy as well. Nature wishes to propagate itself and it does this through the coming together of the male and the female. Despite the fact that ancient Indian civilization was never prudish about sex, it has been swept under the rug. Like an ostrich with its head buried in the sand, many Indians pretend it doesn't exist—it's a taboo subject and for most Indians ignorance is bliss. That a nation which has the *Kama Sutra* as one of its ancient texts is now so prudish about the topic of sex is a mystery, though many blame Victorian morality for it.

While a large part of the world totally avoids the subject, another large part veers towards overindulgence. This is reflected and perpetuated by a media which is eager to profit from its merchandise. Creation, a sacred act, has now become for a large part of the world an act of recreation. Those seeking to extricate themselves from the clutches of narrow-mindedness must guard from going over to the other extreme of licentiousness masquerading as freedom.

At the ground level, closer home in India, the subject of sex is avoided at home and schools as well. A young person only has other equally ignorant peers and other dubious sources of information to learn from. This lack of information and even misinformation extracts its price. We carry our lack of knowledge into the adult world and this ignorance wreaks havoc on individuals, marriages and relationships. Almost all deviant sexual behaviour in society is a result of shame and ignorance about one's body and oneself.

There are signs of hope though. There is a greater awareness about these issues now—a large number of people are becoming more open and are asking questions about sex-related issues, which are answered by doctors, counsellors and experts in the subject in periodicals and other publications and even online. Sex education combined with value education can solve a lot of personal and interpersonal problems, and knowledge about these matters, obtained from the right sources of course, can be a key contributor to human welfare. Doctors and counsellors are available nowadays to impart sex education, and a teacher of yoga and spirituality, particularly one who is married, has faced the challenges of marriage and caters to the householder, should be sought out for value education.

Most people in relationships try to change the other probably because most of us know that changing oneself is a challenging and daunting task. But one who is successful in overcoming one's shortcomings becomes increasingly self-assured and self-confident. A mentally, emotionally and spiritually strong person has more to give in a relationship than someone who is dependent and diffident. The yamas and niyamas of yoga are the don'ts and dos respectively that would make it possible for people to become fuller and better-rounded people. They are qualities many lack in varying degrees, qualities worth cultivating.

YAMAS

Yamas include:

1. Ahimsa (non-violence in thoughts and deeds);
2. Satya (honesty);
3. Asteya (non-covetousness);
4. Brahmacharya (moderation);
5. Aparigraha (non-expectation).

NIYAMAS

Niyamas include:

1. Saucha (purity in thoughts, words and actions);
2. Santosha (contentment);
3. Tapas (effort);
4. Svadhyaya (self-study, introspection);
5. Ishvara pranidhana (surrender to God).

Treat all of the above as instructions in becoming calm, composed and self-reliant.

7

MANAGING EXPECTATIONS THROUGH YOGA

Bhavana had been married for a year and she was quite unhappy. She did her best to do all the things her mother had advised her to do in her new house—she cooked, cleaned, took her ailing mother-in-law out for walks—but she was not happy. She had no complaints about Ravin, her husband. He cared for her, helped her at home as often as he could, spent time with her on weekends, but there was one thing that stuck in her side like a thorn. That one thing was a lack of appreciation. She was unhappy that despite doing so much, her mother-in-law never sang paeans of praise about her in the presence of her friends, and her husband did not thank her often enough for all that she did for his mother and the house. Bhavana expected gratitude and appreciation, but there was not enough of it going around. Result: frustration, anger, tears.

An Indian marriage, like any other, has its ups and downs; one of the ups is that it is not just a marriage between two individuals but between families, and that is also one of the downsides of an Indian marriage. Too many cooks can either make the broth more interesting or spoil it if they are not careful. Regardless of whether a marriage is arranged or on the basis of love, the coming together of two people is like the coming together of two metal utensils—some noise is inevitable. And if it's a joint family, then it's like an orchestra conducted on a range of utensils, and the results are sometimes discordant. It takes time and barrels of patience before any kind of pleasant music can be made from these utensils.

A poet was once asked, 'When should one consider oneself ready for marriage?' The poet replied in his poetic manner that if the husband tells his wife that it is dark even if there is bright sunlight outside, the wife should be ready to light a lamp. And if the wife, in the middle of the summer, says it is cold, then the husband should happily slip into his woollens. A poet's words are not to be taken literally, but it gives an idea of the state of mind required to be ready for marriage.

For the first twenty-five years of life, a person is used to having his or her way. In India, sons are pampered even more, but most people, it can be safely said, are spoilt silly by their parents. As a result, a person who does not even have the skills required to make a cup of tea suddenly finds himself or herself saddled with the gigantic responsibility of making a home. This person who has been the centre of the world, the star of the movie, the one on whom the spotlight has always shone suddenly finds himself having to share the spotlight with someone else. After being in the driver's seat, he has a co-driver and sometimes will even have to ride pillion. The ego's protests begin.

'I always go for a bath first,' the voice inside the newly married man's head says. 'But now she will go first because her commute is longer.' 'My father would never approve of me taking autorickshaws,' the voice in the new bride's head says. 'You can take a cab when your new husband gets a promotion,' the new married voice reminds her. 'I always used to get the best portions for lunch.' 'I have never waited for anyone to see a movie.' 'I don't like to make small talk in the mornings.' 'Why do I have to dress up formally if her parents are coming over?' 'Why didn't he spend time with my parents instead of spending it with his friends?' 'Why do I have to watch the TV serials she wants to watch?' And so on, so forth.

In the first years of marriage, the list of complaints is usually long—there are small problems, there are big problems, there are also small problems that look like big problems. The solution? How does one make a line look smaller without touching it? As mentioned elsewhere, by drawing a longer line next to it. The trick is to become bigger than the problem.

It takes a while to become bigger than the problem; it takes a lot of patience before the two rough egos that have just met, rubbing constantly against each other for many years, smoothen each other to a more malleable state. This may never happen if the partner believes that he or she will change the other over a period of time. A little change may be possible, it is easier when the change comes from within oneself, but to expect a radical change is like buying an Indica and hoping that you will wake up next day to discover that it has turned into a Ferrari. Both partners need to be aware of this, both need to know that they will have to rein in their egos and their expectations from each other. And both will not realize this at the same time. So even if the other does not reciprocate, the one who realizes it first should get started, and may have to go it alone for a long time. Intense love does not measure, it just gives, Mother Teresa once said.

But while you need to plant your feet on the ground, you also need wings to fly. It is better to have expectations of one's own self than of the other person You will never look like Ranbir Kapoor or Katrina Kaif, but it is important to realize that each one of us is unique, and this realization makes it easier to accept the other's individuality and to lay down expectations only for ourselves to which we can aspire to rise. When the young caterpillar was told that he would one day become like the beautiful butterfly that could be seen hovering over the flowers, he could not believe it. He was plain and ordinary, he said to himself, and he would never ever become attractive. But he eventually did. If he had expected other younger caterpillars to become beautiful at the same pace as he did, he would have been disappointed. You may not be able to change some of your qualities, but effort, enthusiasm, energy, application has helped many a seemingly ordinary person to become more productive, efficient, skilled and capable in their professions and lead fulfilling lives. A fulfilled person is able to bring value to a relationship while a physically or emotionally dependent person, lacking in self-esteem, will always put himself and his or her partner in situations that are harmful to the relationship. Bhavana eventually learnt that she, like everybody else, was unique and didn't need anyone to thank her or remind her of how special she was. Bhavana and Ravin's relationship took a turn for the better.

All this learning has to be done on the job. A newly married couple is like two trainees assigned to fly an airplane. There isn't even a manual in sight. To make sure the airplane stays afloat, the two will have to communicate, and this is yet another slippery slope the couple has to learn to negotiate. People mostly talk without thinking, and hear without listening. That the tongue does not have a bone is symbolic of the fact that it is an organ over which most of us have little control, and its waywardness often lands us in trouble. Philosophers and mystics have said that the person who learns to control his tongue can rise to great heights. If a man said to his wife, 'The sugar jar is empty,' as just an observation, his wife may misinterpret it. What did the wife hear? Her husband was chiding her for being inefficient and complaining that she was not looking after the kitchen. She may retort sharply with, 'Why don't you change the bulb in the living room?' This exchange can then be followed by fireworks and explosives. You hear what you want to hear. Harsh words can cut deeper than knives and swords. In the list of yamas (the don'ts) in yoga, ahimsa features before satya. If one has learnt to practise non-violence, then one is qualified to speak the truth. A violent tongue speaking the truth can tear the other person to shreds and cause irreparable damage to the other, to the self and to the relationship.

You can and must make efforts to make yourself worthy of a fulfilling relationship. However, you have to accept that there will always be the X factor, the surprise element in every relationship. You can prepare yourself for it just as you would prepare yourself for an adventure; one always stocks up all the items that one believes will be required for the adventure, but sometimes one may pack a jacket only to find that it is warm and sunny or arm oneself with a T-shirt only to encounter rain. And that is what makes an adventure. Preparation for the adventure and preparedness for the surprises are what makes it fun. You have to know and accept or perhaps learn that things don't always turn out the way you would want them to. You should factor in mystery and surprises.

If you remind yourself time and again that you have, after all, accepted your parents, your siblings in spite of their flaws just as they have accepted you, and it's only a matter of time before this new person in your lives becomes a familiar member of your family, then it becomes easier to accept and assimilate each other.

According to yoga, marriage is an opportunity to find out that you are not the only one around whom the universe revolves. It is an opportunity to learn humility, to learn to walk in another's shoes, to learn to become sensitive to another person's feelings. If you are fortunate enough to become a little more expansive, then it is a chance to learn that others in the world, like the other in your life, are thinking, feeling human beings who deserve to be treated with as much love and respect as you would expect to be treated yourself. The universe revolves around each and every person.

ASANAS FOR SELF-ESTEEM

Motion causes emotion. When feeling relaxed, a person will naturally sit or stand in a relaxed manner. But the converse is also true; it is possible to ease into a state of relaxation if you sit or stand in a certain way. A confident person will generally walk with the spine straight, chest out; similarly, it is possible to invoke confidence in yourself by walking with a straight back and chest out.

While asanas benefit the body, the late Dr Jayadeva added value to them by suggesting that asanas be done with bhavas. Students at The Yoga Institute are encouraged to invoke the feeling of aishwarya while performing Bhujangasana, for example.

BHUJANGASANA

1. Lie on the stomach with legs pointing out, heels together.
2. Place palms on the floor at the side of the chest.
3. Inhale for three seconds as you lift your head and shoulders back without pressure on the palms.

4. Do not lift higher than the navel region while retaining your breath for six seconds.
5. Exhale for three seconds as you return to the starting position.

Featured above are a few variations to practise this posture. These are helpful to include all levels of yoga enthusiasts, the beginner as well as the advanced practitioner.

The asana is not recommended for people with abdominal injuries, hypertension, severe cardiac problems, hernia and colitis.

DHANURVAKRASANA

1. Lie on your stomach.
2. Bend your knees and grasp your ankles from the back.

3. Raise your neck as you pull your ankles from the back. Simultaneously, inhale for three seconds.

4. Retain your breath and pose for six seconds.
5. Return to your normal posture as you exhale for three seconds.

It is not recommended for pregnant women, people with abdominal injuries, cardiac problems, high myopia and piles.

Featured above are a few variations to practise this posture. These are helpful to include all levels of yoga enthusiasts, the beginner as well as the advanced practitioner.

People with high self-esteem and self-respect do not need need validation from others.

8

CONQUERING THE EGO THROUGH YOGA

Geeta was the only daughter of affluent parents and had had a pampered upbringing. Vikas, the man she fell in love with, was a decent fellow from a middle class background. When her parents heard of their plans to get married, they did not give the go-ahead at first because of the different backgrounds and upbringing of the two and the problems these could lead to, but they eventually gave in to their daughter's wishes. Geeta adapted well to the smaller apartment, the differences in lifestyle, but there was one thing that bothered her—picking up the dishes and the plates after meals and ferrying them to the kitchen sink. Her servants had done this for her all her life and Geeta saw it as a lowering of status. It was menial labour and she had a built-in resistance to it. It started off as a small sore issue and developed into a big one. Vikas requested her to go along with it because he didn't see anything wrong with it. Besides, if Geeta exempted herself from this 'menial' task, he would be at the receiving end of taunts from his family about the 'maharani' he had brought home. Geeta did adapt but grudgingly—her pride was wounded—and often taunted Vikas about reducing her to a servant. They managed to limp along like a vehicle with two uneven wheels and a cloud of unpleasantness casting its shadow over their relationship. Geeta did stop nagging over a period of time for the sake of peace at home, but she didn't forget the hurt. It was an uneasy peace; her ego would not let her be.

KLESHAS

In yoga parlance, kleshas are obstacles to happiness. There are five main kleshas.

Asmita or ego is one of the five main kleshas (the others are ignorance, attachment, aversion, fear). Ahamkara, the word for 'ego' in Sanskrit, is made up of aham (I) and kara (maker). The literal meaning is that which makes or causes the I. The dictionary definition of the ego is 'a person's sense of self-esteem or self-importance'. In psychoanalysis, the ego is the part of mind that mediates between the conscious and the unconscious and is responsible for reality testing and a sense of personal identity. An imbalanced ego is capable of destroying people, friendships, relationships; at the macro level, it can wreak havoc on communities, nations and the entire world. Asmita is the identification of oneself with one's ego. One creates a self-image of oneself that one believes to be true, but that is not the case. In yogic philosophy, the ego is essentially everything that blinds one from seeing one's true self. This includes the false perception of seeing the mind and body, which are constantly changing, as the true self (which always remains constant).

In the epic, the Mahabharata, Prince Duryodhana, being vastly egoistic, was not convinced of Lord Krishna's supreme divinity. He only believed that strength of arms, not philosophy, would win him a war—hence he lost.

In the law of the jungle called Matsyanyaya, the big fish

eats the small. But among humans, the strong should protect the weak.

Lord Indra, the god of the heavens, mentions that one can go to heaven if one follows a few rituals like fasting or dipping in the Ganga, but Lord Indra is always under fear that someone will take over his swarga (heaven). Hence, he doesn't allow people to do good or succeed and manages to create obstacles to stop them from becoming stronger.

Then there is another abode, that of Lord Shiva, where there is no desire. Lord Shiva's entire family is totally satisfied and has no desires. And when someone calls out to them for their help, they always render support and guidance to the seeker.

The third abode is of Lord Vishnu, with whom Goddess Laxmi also resides. Whenever Lord Vishnu sees someone suffering, he rushes to help as he undertakes various avatars of Rama, Krishna, Narasimha and Vithal.

As a human, you should make a choice to adapt principles of the higher level. You should learn from Lord Vishnu, the art of helping others and gaining immense joy from it.

How do the above-mentioned anecdotes relate to married life? Well, life is simple and harmonious when a couple is helping each other and not expecting too much from each other. This can become a habit only when the ego is pushed out from the relationship.

Benito Mussolini started a war with Ethiopia for no other reason than 'revenge' for the defeat of Italy in the first Italo-Ethopian war as his pride was hurt. Adolf Hitler and Joseph Stalin, both with massive egos, fought for months over Stalingrad because Stalin wanted to defend his name and Hitler wanted to deface it. Napoleon Bonaparte had a massive ego

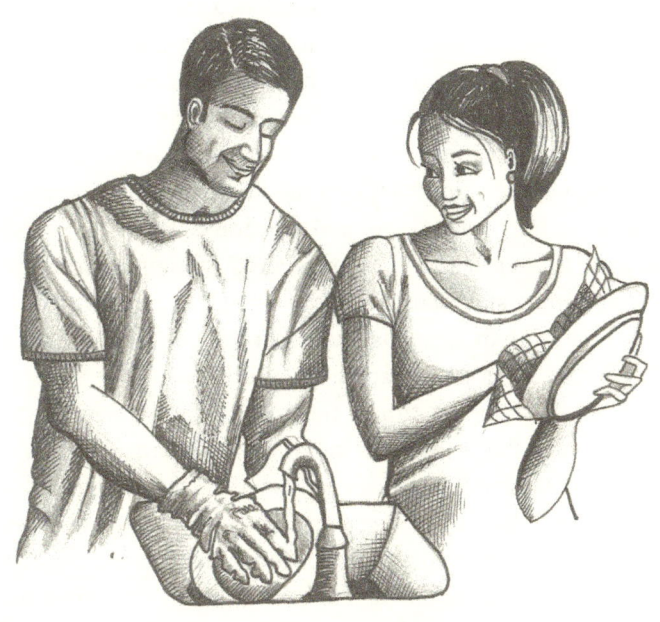

and this so-called great ruler and statesman could not bear the thought of losing at chess and often cheated to win a game.

It is said that Napoleon had an inferiority complex because he was short and he, unconsciously, tried to compensate for his height with his huge ego that drove him on his search for grandeur and led him to wars. Like Napoleon, many of us suffer from low self-esteem, and try to compensate for it by projecting ourselves as other than what we believe we are within. A meek person may try to project himself as a powerful person, a person of limited resources may take a huge loan to buy a car that may make him appear wealthy in the eyes of others, another may drink excessively to impress his friends with his capacity. All these are manifestations of a person who either has a very low opinion of himself or an unreasonably high opinion of himself. Most of us fall in one category or another.

This imbalanced ego rears its head in a relationship in many ways: Do it my way. I know better. Show me some respect. Don't argue with me. I'm the man of the house and this is how things will be done. How come he earns more than you? How come they have a car and we don't? How come their business is doing better than ours? And the competition and the ego games start early in life: I hate him because he got better marks than me. His skateboard is bigger than mine. Her Barbie doll is more expensive than mine.

In these changing times, the role of the woman is also changing and this churns up situations unheard of before. A woman may bring home more money than her husband does and this could become a sore point for both—the man resents it because she earns more and the woman resents her husband because he's not 'man enough' to earn as much. A woman may resent her husband for the fact that his friends have moved up the corporate ladder while he has not. A man may resent the fact that his wife is more intelligent and more successful than him. The ego trip is a slippery walk. Everything is anitya, changeful—social status will change, status among friends will change, designations will change—and pride always comes before the fall, be it from one's position of wealth or of power.

The story of Dvorak, the sculptor, illustrates the power of the ego trap. Dvorak was one of the finest sculptors in his country and was proud of his work and his abilities. When he grew old and it was time for him to die, he decided to fool death with his art. He sculpted eleven statues, likenesses of himself, and hid himself among the statues. When the angel of death came to take him away, he could not tell which one was the real Dvorak. Not wishing to return empty-handed, he came up with an idea to identify the real Dvorak. Standing in front of one of the twelve figures, among which Dvorak was hidden, he exclaimed loudly, 'This cannot be Dvorak's work, it is defective.' Stung by this remark, Dvorak immediately stepped out from among the statues and asked, 'Where is the defect?' That was how he was caught out, the reason being that his ego let him down.

It is the endeavour of all men and women to be equal to all others, and to not be or seem inferior to anyone else. 'Help me, Doctor,' said the patient to his psychologist, 'I have an inferiority complex.' The doctor spoke to him for over an hour, and concluded the meeting by telling him, 'It's not an inferiority complex; you are inferior.' But humour aside, is anybody really inferior? We know the answer to this and every protest by the ego is either meant to restore pride in oneself or an attempt to not be perceived as one who is less than others—and some will go to extreme lengths to restore this balance even if it means hurting others.

TRANSCENDING THE EGO THROUGH YOGA

Whether it's the Napoleons or the Mussolinis waging war on nations, or Geeta and the other men and women waging war on their spouses and the families, it's the ego that drives them to do nasty things to each other. Is there a solution? Yoga is.

Yoga, in a broad sense, is widening one's vision and understanding oneself and the world. Most people understand, or rather misunderstand, yoga or the spiritual path to be one of self-denial, sacrifice, self-restraint, discipline and all other similar words that have now taken on negative connotations.

Also, it is a common misconception that at the end of the spiritual path, the seeker will be transformed into a boring bhajan-singing, mantra-chanter with a halo around his or her head. This is far from the truth. Yoga only points out the route to a harmonious life, and the signboards on this road are honesty with oneself and others, realistic expectations from others, contentment, effort, introspection, transparency, flexibility and other positive qualities.

When a friend of Mulla Nasruddin, a wit who lived in the thirteenth century, asked him how old he was, Mulla replied, 'Forty.' Ten years later, when he was asked the same question by the same man, Mulla, without blinking, replied, 'Forty.' 'But you gave me the same reply a few years ago,' his friend pointed out. 'Unlike other people, I am consistent and stick to what I say.' Unlike Mulla, most of us are just rigid—this can't be called 'consistent' behaviour, and we stick to our views even if the truth, contrary to what we believe in, stares us in the face. We don't wish to lose face by confessing our errors, we fear we would be perceived as weak and fickle, we fail to adapt to changing times. The reality is exactly the opposite. Only the strong have the courage to admit to their mistakes and apologize. Even monks and saints, it is said, have to keep a close watch over their egos, and, often, many who claim to have overcome their egos fall prey to the game of spiritual one-upmanship.

Yogendraji, founder of The Yoga Institute, used to narrate this story about the importance of humility. A large oak tree used to say to the tiny reed growing at its foot, 'Why don't you plant your roots deep into the earth and hold your head high in the air as I do?' 'I am contented with my lot,' the tiny reed replied, 'I may not be gigantic as you are, but I feel safer this way.' 'Safe? You will be safer if you become like me,' the tall, looming tree said to the reed. 'Would anyone dare to yank me by my roots or try and bow my head down?' But the mighty tree soon had to eat its words when a hurricane, raging across the land, tore it up from its roots and broke its firm, rigid trunk into two pieces The reed, bending down to the force of the wind, stood up back again when the storm had passed over.

According to yoga, the person who finds himself will realize his own self-worth. Not just yoga, but all spiritual paths and even the modern understanding of human behaviour, be it transactional analysis or any other tool of modern psychology, lead down this road. Our understanding of ourselves has grown; it's not surprising to see shelves in bookshops full of books on meditation and self-help. The words 'self-worth' and 'self-esteem' are now part of common parlance. Yoga has known this since time immemorial; it's tried and tested, and as it's an integral part of Indian culture, one can and should take advantage of this instead of waiting for endorsements and validations from the West, which is on the journey to discover the self, a journey India completed long ago.

Modern psychology has not reached the root of the problem. Modern psychology talks about interdependence or trying to change each other to your opinions. This is not yoga. Can we expect a dog to behave like a cat and vice versa? No, a dog can only be a better dog and a cat can only be a better cat. It's the same for us humans; each person can only be a better version of himself and cannot change to be like the other.

Yoga works on self-development. Even in a marriage, everything eventually boils down to self-development, self-worth, self-work, self-duty and much more. The process of self-discovery is slow but, sooner or later, everyone has to make this journey into their own selves.

The world population is nearly seven billion and when you look at the mass of humanity that surrounds you, it is hard to believe that there could be anything special about you. After all, isn't each one of us more or less like the other? Each of us has a head, limbs, each has his or her own idiosyncrasies and, therefore, you may wonder if you really matter at all. To make matters worse, the media throws up images of those who have more money, better looks, better clothes, bigger cars and bank balances, and this makes you feel even smaller. When you take a close look at nature, you marvel at the hills and mountains, you are in awe of the beautiful birds, the creatures, and yet you forget that all of us are part of nature. To another species or life form, you may appear beautiful and mysterious. You need to constantly remind yourself of this fact, you need to in fact reclaim your uniqueness. Sometimes you are too easy on yourself, but often you are too harsh. If a friend of yours confesses to a mistake he made, you will advise him to forget it, move on and forgive himself, but if you make a mistake, you are harsh, often cruel and unforgiving to yourself. You have to learn to treat yourself well and yoga helps you in this regard. Once you have the conviction that you are special, that you matter even though you appear small among the people, the mountains, the stars and the skies, it will be difficult if not impossible for a slight or a hurtful glance or remark to sting your pride. It will be difficult to feel small if your partner earns more than you, and neither will you feel humiliated, like Geeta did, if you have to carry dirty dishes from the dining table to the kitchen sink.

If you have the right attitude and outlook, marriage can

be a training ground for learning humility and the art of compromise, for learning empathy and becoming sensitive to another person; basically an opportunity to grow as a person. When you become aware of your own specialness, you also become aware that the other is unique and worthy of respect. A certain amount of openness in communication and transparency with one's spouse can also help one in becoming aware of one's flaws. Perhaps nature meant all of us to be a little flawed to ensure that we would not become vain and egotistic, and to ensure that we would learn humility.

YOGA MUDRA

As mentioned earlier, asanas are practised at The Yoga Institute with an accompanying bhava.

Yoga Mudra is to be practised with the bhava of vairagya.

1. Assume the Sukhasana pose. With your left hand hold the right wrist behind your back. Sit erect. Inhale for three seconds.
2. Exhaling for three seconds, gently bend down and touch your right knee with either the tip of your nose or forehead.
3. Suspend your breath for six seconds.
4. Return to an upright position. Then press back the shoulder blades, inhaling for three seconds.

5. Repeat the same on the left side.
6. Repeat three times, alternately on either side.

7. Having completed three rounds on each side, bend forward and touch the ground with your head between the legs. Hold the posture for thirty seconds and then sit up straight.

This asana is not recommended for people with cervical spondylosis, abdominal injuries, high myopia, retinal detachment and high blood pressure.

Note: Do not expect the asana to bring about miraculous changes in your personality. The feeling of 'letting go' or 'detachment' has to be invoked by the practitioner. Bending forward, the essence of this asana, symbolizes humility and makes it easier to summon the bhava—repeating it will hopefully help the practitioner assimilate the bhava.

9

MASTERING PARENTING SKILLS THROUGH YOGA

At the shopping mall, Neelima had seen an absolutely stunning dress in the shop window and she went into the shop to enquire about it. Neelima had a special talent for spotting beautiful dresses after every fifty metres in the mall. Her husband was left holding the baby, literally. Not that he minded that, but today the baby was howling like an injured rock star and all he could do was hope that Neelima would return quickly from the shop. In the meanwhile, he patted the baby, tried to cheer him up and went on repeating 'Okay, Ajinkya, relax, relax, stay calm.' When a passer-by complimented him on the manner in which he was handling his baby, he was surprised to learn that Ajinkya was his own name and he was only keeping his own cool by reminding himself to stay calm.

Well, the film *Spiderman* had a Part Two and it also had a Part Three, and so does life. It begins when a married couple starts a family—and life changes all over again. Compare it to a company chugging along smoothly or somewhat smoothly, relations between management and labour are cordial, production is high, quarterly results are good and suddenly the company has a new CEO. And this one cries, shouts, screams, has late nights, keeps everyone awake and everyone on their toes. A child is a tough boss to have. This storm let loose in the house, will impact the husband–wife equation, social life, personal life, sex life, finances, eating habits, sleep patterns—every aspect of life—and it will continue to rage for many years. The switch from the joint family system to the nuclear family means the arduous, even though rewarding, job of bringing up the child falls squarely upon the couple, instead of being shared by the large number of members in a joint family, and at times this could stress the relationship.

In the Vedas, it is mentioned that it is a married couple's duty to give at least one child to the world. With a child in their life, the couple becomes more selfless and their journey on the spiritual path also commences. They too grow with the child. Life becomes vast with the universal love pouring in. Our scriptures assert that Pind Brahmand, the entire universe, is your womb. Since new paths open up in a couple's life, the previous measures of happiness change. Gradually, there is less focus on sexual activity and less dependence on each other. Both partners become more self-reliant and giving. Also in a marriage, the focus shifts from the self to the child and his/her healthy upbringing.

A word of caution here: if you are the kind who reaches out to Google easily for your dose of wisdom, be aware that you will find what you are looking for. In the case of Google, believing is seeing; if you search for stories on the negative effects of children on marriage, you will find them, and you will also find enough stories on how children can strengthen bonds between parents. Attitude and outlook are great determinants, and yoga believes that a positive attitude, if missing, needs to be and can be cultivated.

On the positive side, a child is an opportunity for the parents to relive their childhood all over again. If a person is open-minded, then a child can teach his parents to be young once again—to play, to fool around, to live life fully, to be rid of worries and cares. Children can teach parents to reclaim their lost years, and, yes, the lost movies as well. Almost every parent has experienced this—you are watching a suspense film with your wife and infant in a cinema hall. The detective hero has done all his work and is about to reveal the name of the criminal, and that's when your baby starts crying. Everyone around you is annoyed by the wailing and is glaring at you, and you step out apologetically with your wailing baby. Now there is more than one mystery to be unravelled—who is the criminal? Why is the baby crying? When will I be able to return to my seat? Why did I get married and have children? And then in the empty foyer of the cinema hall, your baby suddenly smiles at you. Now you're in seventh heaven. All your questions are answered, and you become a child yourself.

Children help us rediscover ourselves. It's almost as though nature compensates parents, who invested their time and energies in child-rearing, for their efforts, rewarding them for all the nights spent awake for their children, for all the days spent doing homework, for the trips back and forth from the doctor, and other aspects of bringing up a child. But as life becomes more demanding and complicated, people forget this little truth, and try to push their children into becoming like themselves. Sujay's parents hoped he would become a doctor someday. Luckily, Sujay didn't do anything too rash and they got their opportunity to learn from their mistake and realize that

instead of imposing their will on their child, it was important to ask him about his plans. It is important, no doubt, to guide the child, but there is a difference between guiding a boat down a stream and trying to force it to row against the flow. On the day-to-day level too, discipline has to be coupled with compassion; the child should be made aware of his duties; for example, help his or her mother in the kitchen, but discipline has to be balanced with fun. Creating a time slot for poetry, games and sharing jokes balances the serious 'discipline' aspect.

According to Chanakya niti, written in the Arthashastra, the upbringing of a child has to be a mix of love (saam), reward (daam), punishment (daand) and reason (bhed). Parents have to work hard to instil good values, habits and manners in children by adapting these four methods.

The child has to be prepared for the real world which he or she will have to face on his own someday, but the journey to the child's youth can be either a pleasurable one or one laden with stress, and that is always a choice.

The children of most other species take only a few months or a year or two to learn survival skills and fend for themselves. It's only the human child that takes much longer, about 18 to 20 years, to be able to stand on his own two feet. For this long period, parents have to focus all their energies on getting their children to be independent. This is what one has to be prepared for when one decides to get married—total commitment to the family. Bringing up children is a full-time job.

In a world that's on the fast track and changing rapidly every day, in a world that's becoming increasingly challenging, balancing home, work, relationships, friendships, is a tough act, and calls for some skilful juggling. The woman's role is changing, and with both husband and wife chasing careers, as well as the changing family structure, bringing up a child with all the love and attention he or she needs is not an easy task. In the old days, the many uncles and aunts and grandparents in a joint family lent support and the child always had someone to take care of his needs. As families become nuclear, particularly in large busy cities, the third parent—it could be the nanny or TV—starts to play an important role in one's lives. Life in the big, bustling city is a bumpy ride and although there are many challenges, parents would do well to keep some of the basics in mind to make the journey as smooth as possible.

CHILDREN ARE ALSO PEOPLE, JUST SMALL IN SIZE

How would you like it if you happened to be the shortest person in your workplace and your colleagues pushed you around only because of your height? You wouldn't like it. A child is only a short person. A child has a personality of his own, preferences of his own, likes, dislikes, fears and strengths, etc. A lot of them are acquired, and some, if you believe in the soul and its transmigration, are carried over from previous births. Yes, the child might need some guidance in choosing what to do, and this is tricky because guidance can easily cross the line into nagging, nudging and bulldozing; it's tricky territory and has to be negotiated sensitively. In some cases, strong guidance may be required; it will vary from case to case and there are no hard and fast rules. On being asked for advice on parenting, a yogi picked up a handful of sand and gave it to the mother. 'Hold it tight,' he told her, and on doing this the sand started to slip between her fingers. Not good enough. 'Now keep the palm open,' he said. The wind blew away the sand from the open palm. Only when the woman cupped her palm, could she hold on to the sand. Children, like sand, cannot be totally restricted nor can they be allowed total indiscipline; the right mix is essential.

Remember that a sapota (chikoo) tree can only be guided into giving better sapotas, not mangoes.

Let love be the guiding force.

COMPARE AND DESTROY

How would you like it if you returned home one day from work and in the lobby of your building, you saw a list of all the names of the residents and the salaries they draw? Worse, the flats of the people with lower salaries marked with a sign? You would hate that. But parents are often totally oblivious to the harm they cause their children by comparing them, their marks, their talents and skills to those of others. This results in lasting damage and the child will carry this pain with him for the rest of his life; it will hurt him in his career, his relationships, and almost everything he does for the rest of his life. So do unto your children as you would have others do unto you, and, remember, everyone is unique. Again, let love be the guiding force.

One day, Sujay, a twelve-year-old boy, went to his school to collect his examination results and didn't return home. 'Maybe he's catching a late game of football in school,' Ragini, his mother, reasoned. But when there was no sign of him till eight in the evening, Sujay's parents were at their wits' end. They called up his friends, tried to retrace his steps but to no avail. Finally they lodged a complaint with the police. Manas, his father, went crazy driving all around the city looking for his son. At five the next morning, he got lucky. He found Sujay sleeping on a park bench. Manas hugged him, overwhelmed with relief. Sad and scared, Sujay confessed to his father that he had fared badly in his examinations and so was too ashamed to return home. 'I'm just not good at studies,' he told his parents later, 'and I'll never be as good as Rohini.' She was his sister, a class topper. Sujay had been telling his parents that he wanted to learn music. His parents hoped that it was just a phase that would go away and that their son would come around and join the mainstream—but this incident was their wake-up call. They responded to it and today, Sujay is happily employed in the music industry.

PRAISE, DON'T CRITICIZE

For your child, you are Amitabh Bachchan, Aamir Khan, Madhuri Dixit, all rolled into one. When you praise your child, he feels like he is getting an Oscar. And if you criticize your child, particularly in the presence of others, the child's world comes crashing down. Take your child aside instead and discuss how improvements can be made. And praise is not to be reserved only for achievements, but also for efforts. If a child is praised only for achievements, he or she will find happiness only in goals reached. But if a child is praised for efforts, regardless of success or failure, he or she learns that it is worthwhile to invest time and energy in making an effort and success may lie just round the corner. The journey of life then becomes more enjoyable than the destination.

DON'T SAY DON'T

For a child, the world is brand new. There is so much to learn, so much to explore, to touch, to feel, to taste. Adults have been through all this and naturally want to protect their children from anything that can cause hurt. Once again, this has to be done on a case by case basis. 'Don't do this, don't do that' can always be replaced by 'This is how you do it.' There is a fine balance between freedom and restraint, between extreme letting go and overprotectiveness. Both, taken to their extreme, are harmful. If you give your child the freedom to run across the busy freeway by himself, chances are he will hurt himself, but the solution to that is not to tie him up at home. There will be many such occasions where the parent will have to take decisions judiciously and sensitively, although it is easier said than done. If there was a guidebook with rules that could be applied uniformly to all, it would help, but each case, each child, is different. There are no rules and, paradoxically, there *are* rules. It's worth repeating—let love guide you.

ACCEPT, DON'T EXPECT

Doctors invariably want their children to become doctors, actors believe their children will make great actors and a government servant finds it difficult to imagine a career other than a job in the government for his child. And when their children don't live up to their expectations, they are disappointed. Sometimes, when children do live up to their parents' expectations, the parents are pleased, but the children lead dissatisfied lives. If a doctor's daughter did not really want to become a doctor and her heart used to beat for a career in dance, she will not be happy practising medicine. An actor's son wanted to become a software engineer but his parents discouraged him and promised him a bright future in the film industry because they had all the necessary connections, but they should have let him get an engineering degree. There are many such cases; workplaces are full of people leading humdrum lives, wishing they were elsewhere. More often than not, a parent who has chosen his or her own calling, instead of following what his or her parents wanted, will understand if his child wants to tread a different path. Again, there are children who have been left to follow their own calling, have been unsuccessful and now wish their parents had `forced' them to follow a safe path. There is no rule book—mistakes will be made, there will be regrets, but parents should, needless to say, endeavour to do their best.

TREAT YOUR CHILD AS ROYALTY, A STUDENT AND FRIEND

A quote from an ancient Indian text says that a child should be treated as a prince until the age of five, like a student till fifteen and a friend thereafter. It must be understood that when a parent treats the child like a prince, the 'prince' will be treating the parent like an attendant, and when the parent treats the child like a `student', the parent then becomes the 'master' or 'king' or 'queen'. In this way, everybody gets to play all the roles and, finally, friendship equalizes all. A delicate balance has to be maintained between 'friendship' and 'authority'—the child should feel comfortable enough to confide in his parents but not cross the line into disrespect.

TEACH YOUR CHILDREN

You may send your child to the best international school in the country and later to Harvard, Yale, or MIT, but you are his first teacher and your teaching will have the most lasting impression on your child's mind. The child will learn language, maths, biology and other subjects in his school and college, but will imbibe the values that guide a person through life at home. In future, if you find yourself pleased or shocked at the manner in which your offspring behave with you and if you catch yourself asking 'I wonder where he learnt that', there is a very good chance they learnt it from you.

QUALITY TIME VS QUANTITY TIME

'Quality time' has become a popular word because 'quantity

time' is hard to come by. People have become busy chasing their goals, and sometimes, if one is living in a bustling city, it is almost unavoidable. You have little time for yourself, leave aside family and children, and you often console yourself by spending 'quality time' with your loved ones. Most parents try to overcome the guilt of not spending enough time with their families by buying them short-lived means of happiness in the form of junk food, mobile phones, video games and cars, or employ full-time nannies, but these are poor substitutes for the love of a parent. A dinner had together is worth more than the gifts bought out of guilt for children. 'Quantity time' is important, and an environment of trust and caring can only be built if a sufficient amount of time is given to the family. Again, it's a delicate balance and one should take care to see that both parents and children also have their own space.

Just when parents start congratulating themselves for guiding their children through school and their early days, the terrain gets trickier. When the child becomes an adolescent and on the verge of entering yet another new world which is uncharted and always changing, different factors come into play. The opposite sex, dating, love, intimacy and heartbreaks dot this territory. Fasten your seat belts for Part 2 has only just begun. It's time to go to the bookstore and buy that book that will equip you for Part 2, but as you will find out, there are no rule books available because the rules keep changing. There is one new rule though; when the child was young, he or she wanted your approval and would, therefore, try to please you, but as your offspring grows older your approval is not on the top of his list. The child is now on the edge of adulthood, and the approval of peers, the people the now grown-up children will spend the rest of their lives with, matter more than your approval. So if you don't like that new hairstyle or that new pair of jeans, it doesn't really matter because if the friends like it, it stays. Remember that basic rule about love being the guiding force and you will come out fine. And also remember what Kahlil Gibran says in his book, *The Prophet*:

You may give them your love but not your thoughts,
For they have their own thoughts.
You may house their bodies but not their souls,
For their souls dwell in the house of tomorrow,
which you cannot visit, not even in your dreams.
You may strive to be like them,
but seek not to make them like you.
For life goes not backward nor tarries with yesterday.

PARENTING AND YOGA

A game that is played often at The Yoga Institute to emphasize the relation between breathing and the state of mind goes as follows:

Two players are required to play-act, one as a parent, the other as a child. The child has just informed the parent, busy reading the papers or mulling over some business matters, that he has not fared well in the exams. The parent-actor gets upset, resulting in clouds of gloom in the house.

Now the parent-actor is given the following breathing instructions:

1. Sit down in Sukhasana (refer to chapter 4).
2. Relax completely; inhale slowly and gently until comfortable.

3. Exhale slowly and gently.
4. Repeat ten times.

Once again, when the news about faring poorly in the exams is communicated, the response this time from the parent-actor is that of admonishment but gentler, calmer and more balanced. It is almost impossible to lose one's perspective if one has learnt the art of breathing.

Regular practice of pranayamas can make peacefulness a person's second nature, and it is possible for the practitioner, after a considerable amount of practice, to remain unruffled in all situations.

10

ACHIEVING MENTAL BALANCE THROUGH YOGA

Kenny and Priyanka were happily married with two beautiful children. At thirty-two, Kenny came down with a serious bout of depression caused by stress at work. Neither Kenny nor his wife knew how to deal with this, so they fell back on his family for support. Kenny's parents were there for him, but the depression was stubborn and Kenny was not showing signs of recovery. As his ageing parents had their own issues to address, they found themselves unable to keep up with his condition. The entire burden then fell on Priyanka. With two children to look after, Priyanka's hands were full and looking after her husband became tiring. It was a difficult situation to be in and, in addition, they could not comprehend why this was happening to them. After all, they were good people, they lived by the rules, they hurt no one and it made them question all that they had believed in. Slowly, they started to become sad and bitter.

Life often bowls a googly at you and leaves you totally stumped. All of you have plans, goals and ambitions, and when things don't turn out the way you would have liked them to, you are left bewildered. You want to believe that there is order in the universe, there's a method in this seeming chaos, you want to believe that everything happens for a reason. You want to believe that God doesn't play dice, you want to believe in the cause and effect, and yet, seemingly out of the blue, an event will take the wind out of your sails and leave you quivering with fear and wondering what just happened. You want to reject it but you can't. This could be because you are unable to see things from a larger perspective. A story by Rabindranath Tagore illustrates this point well. A young mother was breastfeeding her three-month-old child and, on sensing the child's discomfort due to the awkward position she was in, she decided to shift the baby to the other side. Deprived of nutrition momentarily, the baby started to cry, unaware that in a second both the mother and child would be seated comfortably and return to the feeding routine. Like the child, we too start thrashing and wailing if we are deprived of something that we have set our eyes and hearts on, unaware of the fact that something better might be on its way.

Often, something better is on its way. Often, a situation or an event is nature's or God's way, if you will, of telling us to right a wrong. A toothache has a cause—it reminds you that you may have indulged in sweets and now it's time to ease off. Diabetes may be a reminder that you need to watch your diet and lifestyle in order to bring some balance into your life. Kenny's stress had a cause—he was overworked, perhaps because he was overambitious, and his depression was an unavoidable consequence of his hectic lifestyle. If he had led a life of moderation and balance, perhaps he would have never been laid low by depression. Like Kenny, there are many others who are victims of their own flawed lifestyles; like Kenny, they don't have enough information about the need for balance and how to bring it about, and then when nature comes knocking at their door to set things right, they are totally

flabbergasted. According to Buddha, if you are walking in the woods, and you suddenly find that an arrow has come flying out of the blue and pierced your leg, the first thing to do is to pull out the arrow instead of trying to find out where the arrow was shot from and who shot it.

A lot of our problems are of our own making, caused by unrealistic expectations, an inability to accept flaws in another person even though we may have several ourselves. Our own insecurities are also a source of problems. A person who lacks self-confidence and self-esteem will imagine things that are not there. An insecure and over possessive spouse will imagine slights where there are none, will see demons that don't exist, will suspect the other for no reason at all. When Mulla Nasruddin saw his friend bruised and injured, he learnt that his wife had beaten him up after finding a long red hair on his coat. He warned his friend to be careful, but it was the same situation again the next day as she had found a long black hair on his jacket. 'Now even if you stop fooling around with women, you will get beaten up,' Mulla predicted—and that is exactly what happened. His friend decided he would be loyal to his wife in future, but, after a few days, his wife beat him up when she found no hair on his jacket. 'You shameless creature,' she told him, 'now you have started going out with bald women too!' Often, our problems are in our own heads.

Another common problem is fault-finding. The spouse is either too fat or too thin or too tall or too short. You seek order and harmony in your life by trying to force-fit others into your way of thinking, feeling, looking. You criticize and try to change habits and attitudes others may have had for years with a snap of your finger, knowing fully well that leave aside changing an attitude, changing even an everyday pair of shoes one is used to is so very difficult. Criticism is welcome from one who is perfect, but, fortunately, there is no such person. When the Pharisees wanted to stone a woman who was accused of adultery, all Jesus said was, 'He who is without sin may cast the first stone.' All of them dropped their stones and returned home. Once the sacred vows of marriage have been taken, acceptance of one's spouse has to be one hundred per cent.

In India, and some nations in the Orient, people believe in reincarnation. In this world, others believe that Newton's law of action and reaction also applies to the lives of humans, even after a person passes away. According to this belief, a person has to bear the consequences of his acts in previous lives, and some of your problems in this life may be a result of your actions in your past life. It has its believers and disbelievers, but, regardless, the point to be noted here is that there will be situations in everyone's life when exact causes will be difficult to trace and pin down. They will have to be accepted, and this calls for a certain amount of humility and faith in a higher reality, a belief that nature is trying to set right some imbalances, a belief that this could be for your development. To some people this outlook is second nature while some have to cultivate it in order to face the ups and downs in their lives instead of indulging in self-pity and wondering why it had to happen to them.

The upshot is that there are some problems that you can solve, but there may be some that are out of your control. What does one do if the industry where you are employed in goes through a downturn and you lose your job? What if a bridge collapses and you are hurt? What if you are falsely accused of a crime you have not committed? Accidents, mishaps and other bolts out of the blue fall in this category. The following lines sum up the situation well:

God, give me the courage to change the things I can, the strength to accept the things I can't, and the wisdom to know the difference.

In the case of a married person, the arrow shot at one person injures more than one person; it injures the spouse, the children, the parents, in-laws. There will be ups and downs, there will be unpredictable and unexpected twists and bends in the road, and if you learn to understand and appreciate the institution of marriage, the preparations and sacrifices it calls for, then you are better equipped to deal with the challenges that will certainly face the householder and also appreciate the joys of family life. A householder is equal to a thousand sannyasins, it is said, and the wedding only marks the superficial transformation of a person from being single to being married. The band-baaja-baraat and the horse ride to the wedding venue are only the trailer. Nothing prepares the person for the challenges that lie ahead in marriage. One puts in more effort and work in preparation for a simple school or college examination, but the only advice many receive for this milestone event in one's life is by way of jokes and stories. Sometimes good and genuine advice falls on deaf ears because the young believe they know better, sometimes well-meaning advice is irrelevant because rapid social change makes it redundant. But regardless, a person stepping into the institution of marriage should, at the very least, be made aware that challenges lie ahead. Irrespective of whether the road is smooth or bumpy, the seat belt has to be worn.

A common challenge most couples face after a few years of marriage is ennui. It's bound to happen—a sufficient amount of time has passed and both husband and wife have 'learnt' enough about each other to function smoothly. If it's been plain sailing, there is a tendency for a little complacency to set in, a certain amount of 'taking for granted', perhaps a little boredom and there is a danger of the couple losing interest in each other. This is probably why, in certain communities, the couple gets married to each other once again after ten years have passed by. This renewal of marriage vows is a wake-up call to cherish what one already has, a reminder that the institution of marriage is sacred, an opportunity to sensitize oneself if one has lost one's way down the road and forgotten what it means. Married couples need to remind themselves and each other of what the relationship means to them to keep the fire of love alive.

YOGA SUTRAS

All said and done, despite our understanding of human psychology, physiology, DNA and genetics, etc., the human being is still a mystery, and the deeper one probes, the deeper there is to go. Yoga teaches you to look inwards, and helps you to be honest with yourself and know yourself better. It teaches you to enter your own self with a lamp in your hands. Patanjali's centuries-old *Yoga Sutras* has more insights to offer into the workings of the human mind than modern psychology.

DIFFERENT STATES OF MIND

Pramana

Patanjali states that the human mind functions in five different ways. The first is pramana, which translates to valid cognition. You see everything logically, reasonably and scientifically in your work and do not follow what is not well proven.

Viparyaya

The second is viparyaya, which is misconceptions. In this state, the mind functions in an unscientific manner, based on misbeliefs and superstitions. How many of you tie a nimbu mirchi (stringed lemon and green chillies) to your vehicles? Who stops in the middle of the road just because a black cat has crossed the path? And who considers a sneeze as a bad omen? The human mind is so impressionable that fallacies are followed by many wise people as fear grips the human mind very easily.

Vikalpa

Vikalpa, imagination, is the third state of mind which imagines both good and bad aspects. The choice is yours. For example, if a baby girl is born, a father may feel devastated, as he may have to spend handsome amount on her wedding. However, it could be the other way too. She may grow up to be educated and earn enough to provide support and livelihood not only for herself but her father too.

Nidra

The fourth, nidra, is sleep when the conscious mind is quiet but the subconscious mind is active. Mindfulness helps you to be alert to observe that the subconscious mind holds positive thoughts and doesn't feed on fear and tension.

Smriti

The last state of mind, according to yoga philosophy, is smriti, which is memory. In your memory, you store an opinion based on what you experience about a person. That becomes your reference to form your opinions in the future again when you have to deal with him/her. However, this can prove wrong too. Therefore, you should be alert and learn wisely from your memories.

With the mind constantly juggling between various states, yoga helps you to differentiate between aklishta (positive) thoughts and klishta (negative) thoughts. All of this comes only with practice and detachment (abhyasa and vairagya). Such lessons empower you to master your mind and function effortlessly in life.

When you know yourself better, when you are faced with your own positive qualities and drawbacks, you automatically become aware that everyone else also has his or her ups and downs. This awareness teaches you to accept and empathize, and a broader vision of life teaches you to deal with the vicissitudes of life. Kenny and Priyanka learnt to calm down and be less agitated with the help of yoga asanas and meditation practices. They learnt some life lessons and how to be patient and faithful until the cloud overhead eventually disappeared.

Into every life some rain must fall; everyone will have challenges, that is a given, and the maths ahead is simple—two people will have twice as many challenges and also twice as much joy. According to the Upanishads, what is unpleasant is meant for one's growth, and all that is pleasant is meant to make us happy. In the case of a marriage, understanding each other is possible only if one is able to understand oneself, and even then a hundred per cent understanding of each other may not be possible. A hundred per cent commitment is clearly a better bedrock to base one's marriage on than just understanding.

'The sky is falling!' the duckling cried when a dry nut fell on its head. Other animals heard its cry and there was pandemonium. A wise one among them doubted the veracity of the story and gradually the fear was assuaged. In real life too, one gets influenced by gossip that becomes responsible for our tension. The real answer to many such problems will be to have a balanced state of mind which would allow one to see reality as it is. If one can see things as they are, one can respond appropriately. As Dr Jayadeva mentions in his book *Inspirations*, 'Yoga can help one in becoming well-integrated, objective, calm, clear-headed and intensely concentrated.'

ACHIEVING MENTAL BALANCE THROUGH SARVANGASANA

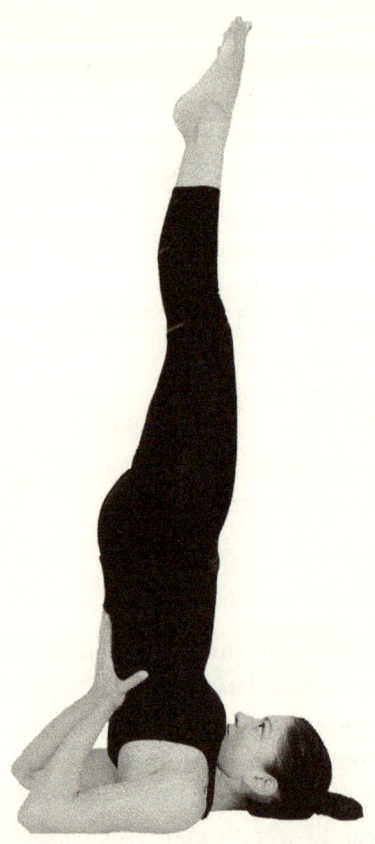

1. Lie supine.
2. Carefully raise your legs up, perpendicular to the floor.
3. Support your hips with your hands.
4. Slowly bend your knees and come down to the starting position, avoiding any jerks.

11

MANAGING FINANCES THROUGH YOGA

Sayali and Manav were made for each other in all respects but one: they were mathematically mismatched. Manav could crunch figures and perform complex calculations in his head while Sayali, a brilliant homemaker with fine taste, was lost even with the simplest of mathematics problems. Manav naturally managed all the finances because of his ability with figures. One day, when he fell seriously ill, Sayali suddenly found herself drowning in an ocean of figures and she was sure she would go under. There were EMIs (equated monthly instalments) to be paid, there was money to be recovered from borrowers as well as credit card bills to be settled. Sayali was totally at sea.

Fortunately, the problem was not of shortage of money, but of excess, so there were no lenders pounding on her door, no bank agents hounding her to pay up. Rich people have different problems. American writer Kurt Vonnegut wrote, 'Rich people are just poor people with lots of money.' That may be true in a certain manner of speaking. 'I'd rather be rich and unhappy than be broke and miserable,' sings a black American rap singer.

In another time, it was possible to romanticize poverty. The wanderer, the mendicant, the hero who would not compromise on his values for any amount of money, were some of the heroes people looked up to. They advocated a simple and austere lifestyle in exchange for peaceful sleep with a clear conscience. Perhaps it was possible to live a dignified life in poverty in earlier days, perhaps one could pluck the fruits off trees and fill one's stomach, and sometimes a helpful friend or neighbour saw the starving hero through. In books and films, the poor hero always managed to find a large leafy tree to rest under, his weary head shaded by it, and sleep a dreamless sleep. But poverty today is crushing. Forget fruit-bearing trees, fruitless leafy trees are also vanishing, and friends and neighbours are busy with their own problems. One has to be wealthy to afford even the basics; a small flat in a big city can set one back by crores.

In the Vedas, it is mentioned that all humans are born different from each other. Hence, your first duty is to know yourself. You must remember that your existence is supported by many other human beings and universal elements. So it is your duty to contribute to the well-being of the world to the best of your potential. Therefore, in the Vedas it is mentioned that every human is supposed to do his purusharthas.

The four purusharthas (objects of human pursuit or self-motivating actions of life) of a human being are artha (pursuit of economic activity), kama (pursuit of sensual pleasure), dharma (doing the right thing) and moksha (self-realization). Although artha is vital to existence, somehow spirituality, over the years, has become synonymous with 'extreme non-materialism'. But is it possible for a householder on the spiritual path to eschew materialism totally? Of course not. The role of money in our lives has changed and we are now living in a material world that we have to learn to adapt to. We must remember that artha makes it possible to live in dharma; honesty is a luxury a poor man cannot afford. In the absence of security at the individual level, living the moral life, and indeed, moksha too, is not possible.

Moderation may be the key to this conundrum. It goes without saying that artha should be pursued within the tenets of dharma, and one should not compromise one's principles, values and morals for the sake of earning a living.

In the case of a married couple, if it's the couple against the world, the problem is of a different nature. But if there are differences between the couple, then financial management becomes a different ball game. The chances of two people being on the same page on the delicate question of money is low; two different people will have different concerns, different priorities. Let's get a car, one might say, and the other will shoot it down, saying it is not necessary because one can always call for a taxi at home now. 'Let's take that foreign holiday' versus 'Let's go to Manali instead because it's as pretty as any foreign destination.' 'Let's send our daughter to university abroad' will be met with 'What's wrong with studying in India?' One could draw up endless lists.

Of course, if one partner is beyond materialistic considerations—a very rare situation these days—the sailing can be smooth, but as in Sayali's case, a sudden turn of events can trip up those who are naive in matters of finance. While the financially savvy partner can and should manage the finances, it is essential in this day and age for everyone to have a basic awareness of money matters. Almost everyone would have come across a widow in movies helplessly trying to make sense of her finances and doing the tiresome rounds of banks and fund houses and courts to put matters of finance and property together. This picture is not far from reality, but it's something that can be avoided if the couple invests some time in understanding each other and their finances.

Excess money can also be a source of distress. As India becomes a developing nation, the problems of excessive money are becoming increasingly visible. Money problems can be compounded by lack of trust in each other or one's fears and insecurities, ego hassles and so on. A society in the throes of rapid social change continues to throw up new and unforeseen challenges, such as in the changing role of women in society, labour unrest and human rights issues and all of these eventually influence the social and economic lives of individuals. A man's ego may be hurt when he discovers that his wife is earning more than him, a woman may be upset when she earns more than her husband or meets his contemporaries who take home better pay packets, in another case one of the spouses might get a pink slip one fine day because the company is going through a downturn. These and other quickly changing scenarios add to the complexities of life.

Anand was not yet financially established as he had just started a new business in the sugar industry. So he told his wife that he would only give her Rs 5, 000 every month and prompted her to manage with that much. To this his wife, Alka, agreed and carefully managed her life and home. Within a year, Anand was well established in his business and thereafter, he always proudly claimed that his wife's unconditional support and cooperation had been the foundation of his success.

Both partners have to learn to be in tandem with each other's duties, needs and expectations. Only then will it be a great and successful joint venture with the deepest understanding.

According to a study by the Kansas State University, having financial arguments is the most common reason for divorce. As unromantic as this may sound, putting money matters in place should take the topmost priority. The following few paragraphs discuss a few things a couple can do to ensure smooth sailing in financial waters.

WRITE DOWN FINANCIAL GOALS

Yoga advocates becoming aware of one's own self, one's own thoughts, and while spirituality recommends living in the moment, it is important for the householder to plan ahead too. Make haste slowly, the wise man said to his student. It is important for a married couple to identify life's goals, prioritize them and then work towards them. If you fail to plan, it is said, it is the same as planning to fail.

OPEN INDIVIDUAL AND JOINT ACCOUNTS

Being practical in financial matters requires having a joint account and an individual account each for a married couple. The joint account can be used for common expenses such as running the house and children's fees, while individual accounts can be used for personal expenses. This is to ensure there is no finger-pointing in case one of the spouses is a big spender and the other is conservative; access to one's own money gives everyone their freedom and also keeps the relationship on an even keel. But one has to be flexible and not too rigid; after all, marriage is a loving relationship and not a business contract. Contributions should be proportionate because one partner may be earning more than the other and it's only fair that the burden is in proportion.

PRACTISE TRANSPARENCY

Learn, slowly if you have to, to speak openly and honestly to each other about finances without hurting one another. Most couples fight shy about speaking openly about money matters, but money matters aren't just about money—they are about how people look at their lives and priorities. Discussing these issues openly will only help bring into focus the issues that need your combined efforts and attention. Burying these matters under the rug won't make them go away. They will only crop up later in an uglier form and have the capacity to ruin an otherwise perfect relationship. Also, communication is important because should one partner be indisposed or unavailable for whatever reason, the other can easily take over. It's like having a co-driver in a car rally.

BUILD AN EMERGENCY FUND

Couples should keep something aside for a rainy day, which could be a medical emergency, a job loss, unexpected expenses for car repair or a spontaneous holiday.

MAKE AND TRACK A BUDGET

A couple should allocate an amount to be spent and an amount to be saved every month, and try to stay within the boundary. Using cash helps a person to be frugal; credit cards tempt you to spend more.

GET OUT OF DEBT AND STAY OUT OF DEBT

It is now possible for anyone with a fairly reasonable income to take a loan and buy a car or a house or a stereo. A purchase can be therapeutic in that it can bring temporary moksha (instant gratification), but it's easy to get sucked into the debt trap and then the person finds that he can never have enough, and has to keep running to stay in the same place. Avoid this source of stress as far as possible and don't give in to impulse buying.

TRUST

All the planning, the prioritizing, the excel sheets, the bank accounts will be of little use if trust, the foundation of any relationship, is weak. Trying to establish a relationship without trust is like trying to get a car moving without the ignition key. One often complains of a lack of trust one has in others and vice versa, but trust has to be won. One of the two, if not both, will have to take the first step and put one's cards on the table to win the other's trust without worrying how vulnerable it will make him or her. It's not easy but as the songwriter wrote, '*Yeh ishq nahin aasaan* (The path of love is never easy)'. There are risks involved, of course, but the rewards are worth every bit.

The couple will also have to work out a policy vis-à-vis their children. Both parents and children have expectations from each other, and keeping in mind the family's economic status, lines have to be drawn. The children have to know clearly what they can and what they cannot expect. Most busy couples, neck-deep in amassing wealth, often tend to spoil their children by giving them too many things instead of giving them their love, time and attention. This is actually a disservice to the children because they grow up being spoilt, badly behaved, dependent and incapable of looking after themselves. If the couple has enough and more, the guiding principle should be: Give them enough to do something, don't give them enough to do nothing.

In middle- and lower-middle class families, the challenges

are of an entirely different nature. Karma yoga, which can come to the rescue, recommends working diligently and honestly at whatever one's line of work is without worrying about the reward. The reward will come but for the present one must keep one's attention on the work to be done and do it as best as one can; rewards will follow just as naturally as effects follows causes. This sort of work ethic, if practised by parents, is bound to percolate down to the children, and stand them in good stead in the future—this is true for persons of any class of society.

In all cases, preparing a will is highly recommended. The absence of a will creates chaos in the lives of the family and often, years and a lot of money are wasted in courts and litigation.

The role of money in the present day should not be understated, but should not be emphasized too much. An extremely flippant attitude towards money and finances is as dangerous as extreme greed for money.

Enter a shopping mall and suddenly, you find yourself surrounded by things you didn't know existed until you saw them and you find yourself wanting them—wanting things that you don't need. In yoga parlance, this could be termed as raga (attachment), one of the five kleshas (the root of suffering). (The others are avidya: ignorance, asmita: ego, dvesha: aversions and abhinivesha: fear.)

Envy, or keeping up with the Joneses, is the other force that drives people to desire and buy things they don't need. A sutra in Patanjali's *Yoga Sutras* advocates the cultivation of positive qualities like mudita. Mudita is altruistic, appreciative joy, the joy of rejoicing in others' happiness, the ability to share the happiness and success of others. Imagine a time that you shared good news of a new job that you are really excited about. When others rejoice in your good fortune, it is encouraging, giving a sense of achievement. When you celebrate the success of others, you express your care for them and you bond with them through love and friendship.

Yoga recommends overcoming raga and cultivating mudita. Besides helping one to sail through life smoothly, overcoming the kleshas and cultivating the positive qualities that Patanjali recommended can also help to counter greed and temptation.

12

STAYING DETACHED AND CULTIVATING FRIENDSHIP IN MARRIAGE

Ragini and Vivek had been married for twenty-five years and, naturally, were used to a certain way of life; they had their set routines, their practices, their way of doing everyday tasks. When Ragini's mother, a resident of another city, had a paralytic stroke, the couple was faced with a difficult choice. There was no one to look after Ragini's mother and they were now faced with a difficult decision—hire someone to look after her or bring her to their home to stay with them. Both were tough options; they felt guilty about leaving her alone, but arranging for her to live with them would disrupt their lifestyle. They were caught between a rock and a hard place.

At some point in your life, you will find yourself in challenging situations with a range of solutions, all of them equally difficult to choose from. Actually, a solution is not so difficult if you are aware of your duties and responsibilities, have honed your ability to discriminate between right and wrong and have cultivated a certain amount of detachment. The most-often quoted example of this conflict between what one wants to do and what one ought to do is the example of Arjuna on the battlefield of Kurukshetra. Arjuna was conflicted because the people he loved, the people who had nurtured him and brought him up, who had educated him and taught him, his close relatives, were now ranged against him on the other side of the battlefield and would be at the receiving end of his bow and arrows. The situation pained him and he wanted to abandon the battle and leave the battlefield. More can be learnt about this from the Bhagavad Gita in which Krishna advises him to put his personal feelings aside and carry out his dharma by slaying those who had wronged him and his family.

DHARMA IS THE FOUNDATION STONE OF LIFE

Over the years, the words 'duty' and 'detachment' have picked up a lot of negative connotations. To many, the word 'duty' implies some sort of punishment that has to be suffered, responsibilities that have to be discharged grudgingly. 'Detachment' is often associated with monks and seekers who have dissociated themselves from society and have chosen to wander in the mountains, searching for some higher truth. It is common to hear about people who have heartlessly abandoned their families and children to pursue spirituality in the name of 'detachment'. Reports about gurus and swamis who claim to be detached but are often caught being attached to ill-gotten wealth and indulging in forbidden pleasures have naturally made people suspicious about the very meaning of the word 'detachment'. In a world where people are already burdened with responsibilities, duty is often something people try to dodge. In the present day particularly, everyone is aware of their rights but few realize that duties are the other side of the coin.

One only has to close one's eyes for a few moments to

become aware of the wild and uncontrollable train of thoughts that speed like a bullet train through the mind. Thoughts, ideas, memories, fears, wants, needs, desires are like a river that has overrun its banks. These are what make one human. You will never hear a dog complain about the rising price of petrol or a bird worrying about the rising cost of education. It is because humans have the freedom to think and desire and also the freedom to abuse, that they need to learn self-restraint, that is, duty and detachment. Should you go to work today or should you bunk and go for a movie? Should you study for your exams or hang out with your friends? Should you spend your pocket money on a book or should you try to multiply it by gambling? Should you take your ailing mother to the hospital today or should you wait for the weekend? Should you divide the profits with your business partner or cheat him a bit because he will never find out?

Your mind is like Kurukshetra, the venue of the war between the Kauravas and Pandavas, and, like Arjuna, you will often find yourself conflicted. And the Kurukshetra of your mind is vast and sprawling; you have duties to yourself, your family, your neighbours, your workplace, your city, your state, your country and the entire world. Ancient India understood the importance of dharma, its most vital role in the smooth functioning of society and the crippling effects if it was neglected. Dharma is the first of the four purusharthas (efforts), the other three being artha, kama and moksha; every pursuit of wealth and pleasure is ill-gotten if it's not guided by dharma, that is, if it's hurtful to others and violates one's own conscience. Yogis hold up the entire functioning universe as an example of dharma; if the earth took a break from spinning on its axis even for a moment there would be complete chaos;

if the monsoon clouds decided to take a holiday in another country instead of coming to India every June, it would be disastrous. For the universe and also for the universe of humans to function smoothly, dharma is the foundation stone. At an individual level, it brings order and stability into daily life, and the chaos one sees today is only because greed has sidetracked humans from their dharma.

DHARMA AND MARRIAGE

Marriage brings in another dimension to dharma. As a single person, it was all right to wander into the cinema hall after a day's work or go out for a meal with one's friends, but for the married person the situation is different. All those are liberties of the past. For a person who is accustomed to being free for more than twenty years of his or her life, this is a radical change which has to be dealt with patiently. The child looks at his old box of marbles and misses the good old days when he spent hours shooting them around with his friends, but the time has come to put it away and look forward to the new joys that lie ahead. With marriage, there will be greater demands on one's time, on finances, on energy levels, and both husband and wife have to rise to the occasion. There will be temptations and distractions, there will be highs and lows, there will be challenges and rewards, there will be, as the film title says, *kabhi khushi kabhie gham* (a bit of happiness and sadness) along the way. Of course, human effort is always directed towards having more of the former and less of the latter, but life never ceases to surprise and one has to be ready and prepared for everything. Digging one's heels in to face adversities requires an awareness of one's duties to one's partner and family.

It is your dharma to keep a balanced state of mind at all times—your first duty is to yourself, your responsibility to yourself, from which you are the first but not the only one to benefit.

FRIENDSHIP AS THE BASIS OF MARRIAGE

It is important to point out here that it's not all just duty and responsibility and adversities and challenges. All this makes marriage seem more like an obstacle course than a happy union of two people, which is how one should view it. When two people come together, the challenges are also accompanied by joys. The spouse is first a friend, and everything is surmountable with a good friend in tow. In the Aranya Parva of the Mahabharata, the yaksha (nature-spirit) asks Yudhishtira, head of the Pandavas, '*Kimsvin mitram grihesatah* (Who is the friend of a householder)?' Yudhishtira replied, 'The friend of a householder is his spouse.' The basis for marriage, according to Hindus, is friendship, and it is this that unites the couple. The following words are uttered by the newly married couple as they take the ceremonial seven steps around the fire:

> *With these seven steps you have become my friend. May I deserve your friendship. May my friendship make me one with you. May your friendship make you one with me.*

To come back to our story: Ragini decided that they would get her mother to come over and stay with them until she was better, and Vivek, aware of his duties as a son-in-law and a responsible husband and caring friend of Ragini's, more than welcomed the decision. It called for a lot of sacrifices on their part, but they did it. Of course, it was not and it's not always duty, duty, duty; Ragini's mother had a great sense of humour and, as she recovered, she helped them recover from their tough day at work with her madcap jokes. If they had not embraced this difficult decision, they would have never found the gem that was Ragini's mother.

Doing one's duty is not enough though. Ideally, one should be able to do it or attempt to do with a positive and cheerful attitude. Being grouchy and sulking while one's mother-in-law convalesces in one's home, taking the family out to the beach and complaining about missing out on a favourite TV show, grumbling about having to watch the soccer match with family instead of friends, are examples of duties poorly performed. Of course, these are examples from day to day life but sometimes the call of duty is far more challenging. We see this often in Hindi films; the policeman father confronting his criminal son often resulting in unhappy consequences, the loving and dutiful mother punishing her son for inappropriate utterances. Situations in films are often exaggerated to make a point, but the fact remains that there will be challenging situations where one will be torn between one's wishes and desires and one's duty. Not only does this call for a sense of duty, it also calls for a sense of detachment.

DETACHMENT THROUGH ANITYA BHAVNA

'Detachment' is a misunderstood word. If a man or a woman is committed to the life of a householder, then neglecting each other cannot be considered detachment; many understand detachment as a painful, self-imposed dissociation from the world around. Detachment, if understood properly, can help us broaden our vision and help us live our lives fully. As mentioned in an earlier chapter, the practice of Anitya Bhavna can aid in the cultivation of detachment, of not being swept away by our circumstances but remaining objective, like a witness, and doing what needs to be done. In the language of cricket it is known as 'keeping one's eye on the ball'.

Regular practice of this technique and a broader world view helps one to cultivate the development of a positive outlook, and enjoy the challenges of life and marriage.

TESTIMONIALS

I have been married to Khatija for the past twelve years. Like every other marriage, ours also had small issues on which we disagreed! I am very meticulous at planning but I cannot honour commitments. This led to a lot of problems with Khatija who decided to take a break and move to another city for a few months though she believed that I was a good person at heart. I felt very hurt when she refused to return. It was then my friends suggested that I join The Yoga Institute's Couples' Class. Initially, I attended the sessions alone but later my wife joined me. After we became aware of the philosophy of yoga we saw things with greater clarity, which helped our marital issues, and our fears and inhibitions diminish to a great extent. We are back together now! I thank The Yoga Institute for this timely support as a stitch in time saves nine!

*Murtuza**

I am married to Rajiv. We live together as a normal couple, but function individually. We have twin sons and have been married for over twenty-five years. My husband is deeply involved in his business and travels often. I did not know how to get him to spend time with me and found myself very lonely. Everywhere I would see couples going to movies, attending parties and weddings, and would feel even more miserable. I husband had neither interest nor any time for us.

---

*All names have been changed to protect the privacy of individuals.

It was then, that I decided to join the Couples' Class at The Yoga Institute. I have been attending the classes for the past ten years, and that too all by myself. The classes have taught me to be a better individual rather than expect my husband to change for me. I've been applying self-development techniques on myself and bettering myself. I am calmer and more balanced now. And it is no wonder that now my husband is no longer reluctant to attend the family meetings. For me, this is a big achievement! Long live the Couples' Class of The Yoga Institute, as it has given me a new direction in life and also made me self-reliant!

Swapna

Mrunal and I have been married for a couple of years. I am a gynaecologist and Mrunal is a psychiatrist. Being well qualified, we both were doing very well on the professional front. However, issues in our marriage started cropping up with the birth of our first child. Though we were ecstatic to become parents, we were not prepared to compromise on our respective careers to undertake the responsibilities of being a parent. Each of us felt that the other should make some sacrifices on the work front to take care of our child. There was so much of acrimony between us over this that we even considered separation as a solution. Thankfully, we were convinced by a friend to undertake counselling at The Yoga Institute before taking the dramatic step.

After numerous counselling sessions, where we were taught the yoga way of life, we were able to strike a middle path for the sake of our child. We realized that our biggest obstacle was our egos. Our journey is the same and there are a few challenges too but now we are able to sail through with

TESTIMONIALS

I have been married to Khatija for the past twelve years. Like every other marriage, ours also had small issues on which we disagreed! I am very meticulous at planning but I cannot honour commitments. This led to a lot of problems with Khatija who decided to take a break and move to another city for a few months though she believed that I was a good person at heart. I felt very hurt when she refused to return. It was then my friends suggested that I join The Yoga Institute's Couples' Class. Initially, I attended the sessions alone but later my wife joined me. After we became aware of the philosophy of yoga we saw things with greater clarity, which helped our marital issues, and our fears and inhibitions diminish to a great extent. We are back together now! I thank The Yoga Institute for this timely support as a stitch in time saves nine!

*Murtuza**

I am married to Rajiv. We live together as a normal couple, but function individually. We have twin sons and have been married for over twenty-five years. My husband is deeply involved in his business and travels often. I did not know how to get him to spend time with me and found myself very lonely. Everywhere I would see couples going to movies, attending parties and weddings, and would feel even more miserable. I husband had neither interest nor any time for us.

---

*All names have been changed to protect the privacy of individuals.

It was then, that I decided to join the Couples' Class at The Yoga Institute. I have been attending the classes for the past ten years, and that too all by myself. The classes have taught me to be a better individual rather than expect my husband to change for me. I've been applying self-development techniques on myself and bettering myself. I am calmer and more balanced now. And it is no wonder that now my husband is no longer reluctant to attend the family meetings. For me, this is a big achievement! Long live the Couples' Class of The Yoga Institute, as it has given me a new direction in life and also made me self-reliant!

Swapna

Mrunal and I have been married for a couple of years. I am a gynaecologist and Mrunal is a psychiatrist. Being well qualified, we both were doing very well on the professional front. However, issues in our marriage started cropping up with the birth of our first child. Though we were ecstatic to become parents, we were not prepared to compromise on our respective careers to undertake the responsibilities of being a parent. Each of us felt that the other should make some sacrifices on the work front to take care of our child. There was so much of acrimony between us over this that we even considered separation as a solution. Thankfully, we were convinced by a friend to undertake counselling at The Yoga Institute before taking the dramatic step.

After numerous counselling sessions, where we were taught the yoga way of life, we were able to strike a middle path for the sake of our child. We realized that our biggest obstacle was our egos. Our journey is the same and there are a few challenges too but now we are able to sail through with full responsibility as we are more aware. Our second child has brought us much joy and now together the four of us make a happy family!

Sudhir

Puneet and I have been married for the past twelve years. Personally, we have never had problems between us, but I always objected to his behaviour towards life and his parents. He was discourteous with his parents and lacked patience. I was worried that he was setting a bad example for our son by disrespecting his grandparents. Being a workaholic, Puneet spent little time with the family. He soon crossed the threshold of obesity, which gave him a lot of health problems. Being an ayurveda charya, I could anticipate these problems. Thankfully, we have been attending the Couples' Class for the past five years. It helped us learn a lot about the importance of following good routines and disciplines. We realized how good physical health translates into good mental health. After attending many sessions of the Couples' Class, Puneet has now altered his attitude and lifestyle and is reaping benefits too. He is working for a better version of himself. This will surely set a good example for our son too.

Bharti

IN GRATITUDE

Writing this book would not have been possible without truly experiencing a fulfilling and rewarding marriage with Dr Saab—Dr Jayadeva Yogendra. He has always been my mentor, guide, strength, close friend and a true companion in all senses.

I want to thank all the individuals who have helped to shape this book. Sadhaka, Mahesh Ramchandani's writing skills reinforced the yogic approach in this book; Deepa Thukral, our dynamic yoga teacher, provided valuable inputs and did the proofreading of the manuscript. Thanks to Aryka Fyzee for giving an insight in the form of credible illustrations and to senior yoga sadhakas, Sharad Waghmare and Priyam Waghmare, for coordinating the couples' classes at The Yoga Institute.

Without the experiences and support from my family, this book would not exist.

I also thank the models, Pramila Khubchandani and Samarth Jani, along with photographer Nirali Manek for the photos of the various yoga practices discussed in the book.

Lastly, I would also like to express gratitude to Jyotsna Mehta, senior editor, Rupa Publications, for her invaluable suggestions.

www.ingramcontent.com/pod-product-compliance
Lightning Source LLC
Chambersburg PA
CBHW032000080426
42735CB00007B/455